DOUBLE
DESIRE

DOUBLE *DESIRE*

A FOURPLAY NOVEL
GEMMA BLYTHE

If you'd like to know if this book contains any elements that might be of concern for you, please check out the following webpage for details:

https://www.gemmablythe.com/content-notes

To all of us with a later in life bi awakening—may we always remember that we count.

Part One

Chapter 1
March

THE FACT THAT MY best friend Bex messages me during our kids' fifth-grade band concert isn't really a surprise. If you've ever been to an elementary school concert you know what I mean, and since our kids were up first, we now have another thirty minutes of listening to other people's kids. Texting is a more socially acceptable way to pass the time than falling asleep on your wife's shoulder, like the guy a row in front of me.

The surprise comes from *what* Bex sent me.

> *Bex: Rafe's and my anniversary is coming up next month. Sixteen years!*

I know this, seeing as I was the maid of honor at her wedding. She was the matron of honor at mine, two years later. Being best friends since the first day of college will do that to you.

> *Me: You doing anything fun?*

> *Bex: Still deciding how we want to spend a kid-free*

we want to spend a kid-free vacation. We'd toyed with the idea of just going somewhere in the hill country, get an airbnb or something.

The dots appear and disappear, like she's either taking a long time to type something, or typing and then deleting. Finally, a message comes through.

Bex: Would you guys be interested in joining us?

When I read the question, all the air leaves my body, because the immediate answer is yes, absolutely yes.

But then I wonder if she's asking what I *think* she's asking.

Last September we went on a vacation, just the four of us, and I don't think any of us were expecting it to go the way it did. In the six months since, we've only talked about it once, and that's when we decided to never talk about it again.

Don't get me wrong, it was fun. It was a *lot* of fun. But it was also the kind of thing that could have totally fucked up our friendship if we'd let it get out of hand. That's why ending it when we came home was the only logical choice.

Which is why I'm both intrigued by and uncertain about the invite.

I glance over my shoulder at her, and she's staring back at me, though when our eyes meet she turns beet red and looks back at her phone. Which, fair enough. I'd have probably done the same if I'd been the one to ask and she'd tried to turn it into an in-person discussion.

Bex: Oh my God, don't look at me, I'm asking you here instead of in person so that we can pretend like I never asked if we need to.

Me: Are you asking what I think you're asking?

Bex: I'm going to go out on a limb and say that it depends on your answer.

Bex: For plausible deniability.

Me: I mean, I have to ask Alec.

Bex: Okay.

I nudge my husband, who's reading the program like it's a novel, and just as I tilt the screen towards him, Bex sends another message.

Bex: Not right now!!!!!

I snatch the phone back, about to ask why she asked *me* right now if I'm not supposed to ask *him* right now, when my phone vibrates with another message. This one's from Alec to the group text we share with Bex and her husband.

Alec: Darcy & Bex, something you two want to share with the rest of the class?

That's when the song the current kids are singing ends and everyone starts clapping. I put down my phone and join in, thankful for a distraction from the fact that I was just trying to negotiate an orgy while sitting in a school auditorium.

***

After the concert we mingle with other parents, waiting for the kids to come out. As the PTA president, tons of people have questions for me, but eventually we make our way to Bex and Rafael.

"You never answered the text," Alec says, wrapping his arms around my shoulders from behind. "What were you two being so secretive about during the concert?"

Bex turns bright red when our gazes meet.

"Text?" Her husband asks, but when he looks at Bex they have a silent conversation, and realization dawns on his face. "Oh. Wait, you asked Darcy *here*?"

"I feel like I'm missing something," Alec says, so I wrap my hands around his forearms and give him a light squeeze.

"Their anniversary is coming up, and they were wondering if we wanted to join them on a getaway."

I keep my voice light because we're at a school, surrounded by other parents, and our kids are coming out at any moment. But I can tell by the way he goes still behind me that Alec knows exactly the meaning behind the invitation, and when I turn to look at him, he's looking at Rafael with definite heat in his gaze.

"Ye-," he starts, then freezes and looks at me to check in. It reminds me of that last trip, when we both wanted so much but also wanted to be sure the other one did too, how we always put our own relationship first. "I mean..."

I give him the briefest of kisses. A quick conversation with our eyes and tiny nods, and I can tell he wants to. I know *I* want to. So I look back at Bex and Rafael.

"Yeah."

***

You'd be forgiven for thinking it's weird that my husband could watch Bex go down on me, that I could watch her husband go down on mine, that we could have a simultaneous 4-way orgasm in the shower, and continue to be friends afterwards. To be honest, if you'd told me before our vacation that it was possible, I'd have thought your story was totally unbelievable — hot, yes, but not tethered to reality. But somehow it worked for us.

We still hang out all the time, our kids are all friends, we even went on a joint family vacation over spring break. The only real difference is that Bex and I don't share the dirty details of our sex lives anymore. I miss it — she's been there to gossip about my sex life since before I had one — but it would bring up too many memories. Mentioning the mind-blowing bedroom session Alec and I had last week would probably result in both of us remembering how she had me spread out, naked, on the bed of that rental, guiding my husband's fingers in my pussy and showing him where my g-spot was. And that's a memory better saved for alone time with my vibrator.

They taught us the fun of g-spot play, and we taught her how to deep throat. It was a very educational vacation and I hope they've used what they learned even half as much as we have.

I also wonder if they think about us sometimes. I wonder if, after a few drinks, they talk about us while they're fucking, tell each other to pretend like we're in the corner, watching them. Does Bex ever tell Rafael that she imagined my hand when she was masturbating? Does Rafael ever tell her that he imagined Alec's? Or are we the only ones that occasionally invite them—or at least the memories of them—into our bedroom?

Well, they invited us on the trip, so I guess we've come up at least occasionally.

Chapter 2

"Was tonight the first time she brought it up?" Alec asks as we're getting ready for bed that night. That I know exactly what he's referring to speaks to how much it's been on my mind.

"Yeah." I'd have told him if she had. I figure he'd have told me the same, though I feel the need to ask. "Rafael ever bring it up?"

Alec shakes his head. The guys don't hang out nearly as much as Bex and I do, but they play in a recreational soccer league together every spring, so the past couple of months they've been spending more time together.

Stripped down to his boxers, he crawls into bed and I drape myself across his chest. For a minute we're silent, his fingers fondling the thin strap of my negligee, and then he pulls it down my shoulder and plants a kiss against my now-bare skin. "I wasn't too eager, was I?"

Chuckling, I shake my head. "I was just as eager when she texted, though I told her I needed to check with you first."

"If you didn't want to, I wouldn't. I won't, I mean. You still have plenty of time to change your mind."

His fingers play with my hair and I wonder if he's nervous. Nervous I'll back out or nervous about what might happen or maybe both. When we talked right after our last vacation we chalked it up to a one time thing, so aside from bringing it up during sex, or after a few drinks or a gummy, we haven't really discussed it. No reason to prepare a party-line answer for a question you don't think you'll ever be asked.

But now that we *have* been asked, I'm really, really glad we're on the same page.

"Same," I breathe. Because, God, I want Bex's fingers in me so bad, and I want to taste her again, but Alec and the life we've built together will always come first.

His body sags with relief, so I know he's not planning to back out either. And suddenly I'm bursting with excitement that has some nervousness around the edges. Because I can't wait, but I also can't believe it. Last time we managed to not fuck our friendship up, hopefully doing it a second time isn't flying too close to the sun.

Hopefully, taking down this platonic wall we've built over the past six months won't ruin everything we've worked so hard to normalize.

Hopefully it will be fun and good and sexy and absent any stress or complexity.

It will, right?

When my mind is racing with what ifs, Alec helps me focus on the present, and we both need that right now. So I crawl on top of him, straddling his hips.

"Sounds like we're doing this again?"

He nods, his warm hand wrapping around my neck as he tugs me down for a kiss. I take long pulls of his mouth, sucking on his tongue, and he presses his hips up so that I can feel his cock against my pussy, right where I want it.

"God," I groan, starting to rock my hips against him, and Alec reaches for his phone to turn on the music so the kids can't hear us. The oldest one probably knows what this playlist means by now, but it's still the polite thing to do.

With a grin Alec sits up and pulls my negligee off, and before I know what's happened, I'm on my stomach and he's the one kneeling over me. Then his breath is hot against my ear, his voice a growl.

"This what you had in mind, love?"

I nod and he drags my underwear down with his teeth and then parts my cheeks with his hands, exposing me to him. There's a pause, and I wiggle my ass, earning a throaty chuckle.

"Do you want me to eat you out or something?"

Propping my head up on my hand, I squint back at him. "I mean, if you're offering, far be it from me to—"

But I'm cut off when he slides an arm under my pelvis, hiking my bare ass in the air, and I feel the warm wet of his tongue flat against my clit.

Dropping my head against the bed, the sheets muffle my moans as Alec travels from my clit to my pussy. "Fuuuuck," I say, rocking back against him eagerly.

He's not in any rush, though, taking his time, flipping us so that I'm sitting on his face. I look down, our eyes meeting as his tongue works me over, and then a finger joins, sliding into me. I clutch at his hair, and the groan he makes in response vibrates through me.

A second finger joins the first as his tongue draws lazy circles on my clit.

Over a decade of marriage has made him a talented multitasker, and soon I'm ready to beg for his cock. Or would be if I could make any sound other than the needy gasps that are currently escaping.

Eventually he shifts me off him and settles behind me, hiking my ass up again and positioning himself at my entrance. A slow circle, then he pumps himself with his hand, lubing himself up with my juices.

"You ready for me, baby?"

I nod

"Good."

A quick thrust and then I'm full of him, and it feels so good I don't even care about the inelegant *ugh* that escapes.

Alec starts thrusting in and out, small movements at first, but then they grow. A hand wraps around my hair and he tugs me up, hauls my back against his chest as he gropes one breast, then the other.

"Good, baby?" he asks, and I nod in case the whimpers aren't confirmation enough. Reaching down, I slip my hand between my legs and through my slick folds. My clit is swollen and needy and I rub it frantically as Alec rolls a nipple between his thumb and forefinger.

"These tits," he says when I gasp. "That ass," he continues, giving one cheek a slap, hard enough that I know there'll be a faint pink hand print when we're done. Then the backs of his fingers drag up my torso gently. "This body."

The sting followed by tenderness keeps my nerve endings on edge, amps up the sensations as he strokes me from the inside and I match his movements.

His other hand is still wrapped around my hair, and he turns my head with it, kissing me gently.

"Do I really get you forever?"

I nod again, and he kisses me again as his thrusts become more erratic. The tingles all over my body settling as my orgasm begins to build.

Another rough tweak of my nipple and I'm right there, teetering on the edge.

"Fuuuuck," I groan.

Another tug of my hair and then, "Do it."

He almost always times this order perfectly, and tonight is no exception. I come and every one of his thrusts is another shock of pleasure. Just as I finish, he comes, buried deep in my pussy, body jolting from his own mini shockwaves.

We collapse on the bed, sweaty and spent, a light sheen covering both our bodies as our playlist continues in the background.

"You're not half bad at that," I say with a smirk, and he laughs, pressing a kiss to my shoulder.

"I've never gotten any complaints."

Chapter 3

A COUPLE OF WEEKS later, I have my annual and my doctor asks if I'd like to add an STI panel to my tests this year. When I started seeing her, she let me know this was a question she asks all her patients every year, regardless of relationship status, and it's always been an automatic no until today.

"N..." I start, then frown. Do I?

She looks up, face unreadable, so I take a deep breath.

"If a woman went down on me?"

She nods. "I'd recommend it, especially if you don't know what her testing status is."

I mean, I hadn't thought about it, but I have no reason to think Bex's status would be a question. Or that Rafael's would be, for that matter. I can't imagine either of them cheating on each other, but what if they didn't cheat? What made Bex and Rafael decide to ask us on another vacation? Have they done it since? Maybe we unlocked some kind of new kink they've been exploring.

Suddenly, I'm wondering if we're the only couple they've done this with and I'm feeling a little ill.

"I'm assuming testing me would also catch anything my husband might have? If we've had unprotected sex since?"

"More than likely, though I can give you some places he can get tested as well, if you'd like."

An hour later I walk out with a list for Alec and an upset stomach. Once I get in my car, I pull out my phone to text Bex.

Saw Dr. Haun today and she asked if I needed to get tested and I realized I didn't know the answer to that? And that we should probably talk.

My phone shows Bex is typing, but then stops, and my phone rings.

"Sorry," she says before I can even say hi. "Javi keeps stealing my phone to play some stupid game on it, so I thought we should avoid leaving a paper trail with this conversation. But no, I don't think you do? Unless you'd feel better about it, obviously. I'm not going to talk you out of it if you want to."

"I went ahead with the test, because I figured why not. Suddenly I wasn't sure if you..." My voice trails off because I'm not sure how to ask my best friend if she and her husband have hooked up with other couples.

"We haven't," she starts, then stops and clears her throat. "Wait, have you?"

"No!" I say, more offended than I should be, considering I was just asking her the same question.

Though, to be honest, it probably would make more sense to hook up with some random couple that we found on an app or something. It would be way less complicated, run a way lower risk of blowing up our friendship.

But the problem is, I don't *want* to hook up with some random girl. I want Bex. And Alec and I haven't talked in those kinds of specifics, but I'm pretty sure he wants Rafael. Though now that we're doing this again, we *should* talk in those kinds of specifics.

"You're our first," I tell Bex, quietly. "Our only."

"Same," she says, and I guess my sigh of relief is audible, because she adds, "Darce, you're the first new person I've kissed since college."

Reassurance floods through me that we're all coming at this from the same place.

"I don't know. You guys could have checked out the scene after last time or something."

"I think that would have felt like cheating," she says a little hesitantly. "Wouldn't it?"

"It technically wouldn't have been," I say, even though that's exactly what it would have felt like. "We didn't have some kind of exclusivity conversation."

"Should we?" she asks, and I pinch the bridge of my nose. This is getting complicated. Last time we didn't do all this, we just made out. And then had sex. I don't *want* to have to do all this extra stuff.

"I don't know? At the very least, we should involve the guys in this conversation."

"Okay. Maybe we can do it on the trip."

"Yeah," I say, then hear a commotion on her end.

"Does your mother know you're here?" she asks, and then a very familiar voice says, "I don't know?"

"Hey Darce," she says, and I can hear the laughter in her voice. "Do you know where your oldest is?"

"I have some suspicions. Put me on speaker?"

"Hi mom." My fifth grader, Jimmy's, voice comes through the phone. "Caught the bus home with Javi!"

"If you want to play video games with your sister tonight, please do your math homework before Dad picks you up."

He grumbles, and then I hear Bex tell them to go upstairs and she takes me off speaker.

"He wasn't expecting me to be talking to you when he walked in," she laughs.

"He should know better by now. They all should, really."

"Yeah." Her voice lowers, and then she continues. "I'll get tested, and Rafe can too, if you want."

"You don't have–" I start, but she cuts me off.

"If we're going to do this, I want to do it right. Last time it came out of nowhere, but if we're going to be more intentional this time, then let's do it the right way."

My heart starts pounding in my chest, because this *is* intentional. Deliberate. I don't want to think too hard about whether that means something. And if so, what.

"Let me talk to Alec? And you talk to Rafael. Just testing you and me is fine for me since we'd theoretically have the same results as the guys, but if you or either of the guys want–"

"I'm good, but I'll check with Rafe."

"Okay. I'll talk to you later then?"

"Yeah." She's silent for a moment, then adds, "I'm really looking forward to the trip, though. Rafe and I found a place that I think will be tons of fun."

"Gonna send us a link?" I ask.

I can hear the grin in her voice when she answers, "Nope. It's a surprise."

Chapter 4
May

I DON'T KNOW WHAT to pack for a swingers weekend with my best friend.

Alec finds me in our bedroom, surrounded by lingerie, sex toys, and an empty suitcase. He wiggles his eyebrows, then throws me a wink. "Packing for ourselves is going to be way more fun than packing the kids for their grandparents."

"It's not fun, it's stressful!" I say, slingshotting a bra at him.

He catches the small scrap of lace and mesh, inspecting it. It's new, something I bought last week on a whim, and I've been trying to decide if I should take it. Or am I supposed to save the new stuff for my husband's eyes only?

But Alec grins, dropping it in the suitcase. "This is definitely a take."

Flinging myself to the ground, I watch as he stretches out on the foot of the bed, facing me.

"Does it feel weird to you this time?" I ask.

"How so?"

"Last time we accidentally stumbled into this. We didn't go on vacation planning on swapping partners. But this time we are... I don't know. It just feels different."

"Are you having second thoughts?" Alec asks, and I shake my head more confidently than I feel.

"No. I mean, I'm looking forward to this. I really am. It just... feels weird."

It's hard for me to put into words exactly how I feel, especially because I don't want to make it sound like I don't trust Alec. Or Bex, or Rafael. But being intentional about this by planning for it and getting STI tests is different. I've been lurking in a swinging subreddit, for fuck's sake. It's different.

I want to spend more time with Bex. Even though we only spent a few days being intimate, I've missed it. I want to hold her and touch her and kiss her and make her come. But this isn't something I ever expected to do, it's not a turn I expected my marriage to take.

"If you change your mind," he starts, but I cut him off.

"I won't. It's fine. Different from last time, but different isn't bad."

He nods, but doesn't say anything, rolling onto his stomach and studying me. Desperate to change the subject, I reach for one of our toys and hold it up, then toss it at him. "Take, or leave behind?"

He studies the hot pink butt plug, a sly grin crossing his face. "You think they're into anal play yet?"

"I have no idea." And I miss that part of our friendship, too. Not talking about sex with Bex is weird.

"We should take it," he declares. "If they're into anal, then great. If not, but anal curious, then maybe we can walk them through it."

I laugh. "Walk them through it, you say?"

He nods, sliding on the floor to join me, and then reaching for the bottle of lube among the sex toys. "Show them how it works."

"How to prep for it?" I ask and he nods, rolling me on my back and pulling my shorts and underwear off before resting my feet on his shoulders.

"The importance of going slow," he says, drizzling lube on a finger and then sliding his finger in my crease. He probes my back entrance, but just teasing, and after a minute I've had enough and shift my hips towards him.

He grins. "You want something?"

"Your finger, if it wouldn't be too much to ask for," I say and he gives me it, sliding past the initial ring of muscle as my body welcomes him in.

"Mmmmmm," I sigh lazily, the sensations decadent as he slides in and out. "That's..."

"Good?" he asks, and I nod, my eyes drifting shut as a second finger joins the first.

Now there's stretching, and he adds more lube before slipping in a third finger. A fullness, as he preps me for his cock.

"We'll show them there's nothing to be scared of," he says, leaning over to press a quick kiss to my mouth. "Bex will see you blissed out like this and she'll be begging for Rafael's cock in her ass."

I rock against his fingers, sliding one hand between us to play with my clit as he explores me from the inside.

"How about yours?" I ask, reaching blindly into the pile of toys behind me. My hand clasps around the one I'm looking for, and I hold it up for him. "You want to show them how hard you come when you have this in your ass?"

He grins and nods, opening the bottle of lube one handed and drizzling it on the vibrating prostate massager as he continues to work me open with his other hand.

"You may have the honor," he tells me, shifting forward a bit so that I can reach his ass. His mouth covers mine as I reach behind him, locating the spot I'm looking for and slowly slipping it in.

He groans against my mouth as I penetrate past the initial tightness and slide the toy into place. When I turn the vibrations on, he groans again, louder.

"Darce," he moans, and I grin as his eyes roll back in his head.

"Don't forget to fuck me," I tease.

Alec gathers himself enough to pull his fingers out, giving his cock a couple of lubed-up pumps before positioning himself against me. A sudden thrust of his hips and then he wraps his hands around my upper thighs and pulls me closer, until he's fully seated in my ass.

It's everything. It's fullness and completeness and tightness and wonderfulness and everything.

One slow pump, and then a second before he starts speeding up. I can tell from the way his brow furrows that he's close, that the toy in his ass is bringing him to his peak quickly and he's trying not to beat me to orgasm. His hips slam against me, and he leans forward, mouth closing around one of my breasts, then the other, teeth scraping my nipple. My own hand works my clit furiously as my hips cant up towards him, straining for my peak.

And then suddenly I feel it coming on me like a wave, and it can't be stopped. My fingers on my clit and his cock in my ass and his teeth against my nipple all meld together.

"Fuck," I groan, but it's all I can say before it takes me over, the pressure releasing in a storm of sparks and vibrations.

"Darce," he grunts just a moment later, coming as he buries his face in my neck so that his own sounds don't draw any more attention to our room than we have already. His teeth scrape against my neck now, the sting of it amplifying all the other sensations coursing through my body.

He collapses on top of me, pressing me into the floor, and we're both panting. We lay there, tangled until our breath turns to normal, and then Alec stands, going into the bathroom and returning a minute later with a wet washcloth.

"Think we can sell it?" I ask with a grin as he cleans me gently.

"If not the first time, we'll just have to keep demonstrating until we do," he says with a wink, then collapses on the floor next to me. He turns his head. "Hey, did you butt dial me earlier?"

I frown, shaking my head. "I don't think so. Why?"

The smirk he puts on is irresistible. "Because I swear, your ass is constantly calling me."

I groan and laugh and shove his shoulder lightly. "The worst!"

Shaking his head, he shifts so that he's hovering over me, weight on his forearms so that we're not touching. "The best," he says, then gives me a quick kiss.

Chapter 5

Bex and Rafael stay tight-lipped about the place they rented, so by the time the day comes around I'm equal parts excited and nervous, a near-constant tingle of anticipation running through me.

"*Now* will you tell us?" I ask as Alec and I slide into the back seat of their car.

"It's like a one hour drive! Patience!" Bex says with a grin. "Here's a hint, though. We did *not* find it on AirBnB or VRBO or any of those other standard sites."

Alec and I glance at each other as we try to parse that out.

"Is it a kinky place?" Alec asks, and Bex just shrugs, a smirk lingering on her mouth.

Fuck. We're still within city limits and I'm already thinking about tasting her.

Rafael clears his throat. "Bex did some reading beforehand, and thought it would be good to talk about boundaries, anything we'd like to try, or anything that's off the table."

I nod, and Alec reaches over for my hand, squeezing it. We talked again about how this time felt different, and this is the perfect example of why. *Talking* about it feels so much more businesslike than just *doing* it.

But everything we've read supports what Rafael is saying. And we've discussed what we're okay with and what we're not into as well. So we're prepared for this conversation.

"I liked everything we did last time," I start, and it's the first time we've ever discussed this with them, which is actually kind of hot. "Watching y'all fuck, y'all watching us fuck. Bex, everything we did—making out, fingering, oral."

"This place have Twister?" Alec asks. "Because I'd be down for drunk naked Twister again."

I laugh. "Last time we were neither drunk nor naked."

"Fine, tipsy bathing suit twister," he corrects with a grin.

"The shower was great," Bex says, and my pussy clenches at the memory. Jerking off Alec while Bex points a shower head at my clit and Rafael fucks her.

"Please tell me this place has a good shower situation," I say, and Rafael and Bex exchange a heated look and grin before Rafael glances at me through the rearview mirror.

"I think you'll like the bathing options."

I grin and clap my hands, bouncing in my seat. "Yesssss."

Bex laughs and rolls her eyes.

Alec grins. "We brought toys. Mostly vibrators and butt plugs."

Rafael clears his throat, and now glances at Alec in the rearview mirror. "I, um, don't think I'm up for anal yet."

Alec doesn't seem to mind, nodding and telling him that's totally fine, but my mind caught on one of the words Rafael said.

Yet.

Yet implies more. It suggests that Rafael doesn't want to have sex this vacation, but that he might be up for it on a future vacation.

Holy shit, are there going to be future vacations with them? Could this become a thing, the four of us taking off together for childfree weeks? Or even just weekends, cramming as much debauchery as we can into a few days, going on an orgasm bender every once in a while?

God, just thinking about it–I really fucking want that. I'm not sure I'll ever get enough of Bex, and if we're opening the door this trip, I don't know if I'll ever want to close it.

We probably need to get through this week before I start thinking like that, though.

"...anniversary gift," Alec is saying.

"Pictures?" squeaks Bex, and she and Rafael glance at each other.

"Only if you guys feel comfortable with it. My camera can stay in the trunk the whole trip, if you want. Or I can take G-rated, living room-friendly pictures."

"If you ask me though," I butt in, "he should take pictures of you fucking."

"Darcy!" Bex exclaims, and she's blushing, but her nipples are poking through her shirt. Which means she at least sees the appeal of the idea. And after months of trying to pretend I don't notice her obvious tells when it comes to being turned on, I finally get to acknowledge it again. With a grin I point at my own tits, and she looks down and covers hers with her forearm, mouthing *shut up* at me.

"Do you guys have pictures like that?" Rafael asks, and Alec nods.

"I've taken approximately a million pictures of Darcy in lingerie and naked, because have you seen her? How could I not?" I preen at that, then reach for my phone to log into the secure photo and chat app we have. "And a good number of us fucking."

"This is one of my favorites," I say, passing it forward to Bex. "And it doesn't even have our faces."

It's a black and white photo of Alec sliding into me as I straddle him. He held the camera near our heads, so it's a birds-eye view of what we see when we watch ourselves fucking. It's erotic and—if I do say so myself—we look totally bangable. But it also looks kind of artsy.

"Damn," Bex breathes, then holds it out for Rafael, who glances quickly, and then does a double-take before focusing on the road again. He reaches over and places his hand on Bex's knee, then slides it up slowly. "We'll talk about it and let you know," she says as she hands the phone back to me, and when I wiggle my eyebrows at her, she blushes and laughs.

"But seriously, no pressure if you pass," Alec says, and they nod.

"Anything else we need to discuss?" Bex asks, and when I glance at Alec he shrugs so I do too.

"We're good for now if you are. Obviously we keep checking in with each other, whether it's to confirm or change or add or take away or whatever," I say, and Rafael and Bex nod in agreement.

"Can you pull out the directions again?" Rafael asks Bex. "We're getting close."

Chapter 6

IT WOULDN'T SURPRISE ME to discover that the place we're staying has been used in porn shoots. I don't know how many adult films they make in the Hill Country, but if they do, this is where they do it.

Three bedrooms with huge beds, a shower you could definitely fit a film crew into, and a bathtub the size of a hot tub.

"Where did you *find* this place?" Alec asks, and Bex grins.

"A website that caters to people in the lifestyle. Most of them are BDSM-focused, with *50 Shades*-style dungeons and everything, but this one isn't that hardcore. Still, we thought we could have fun here."

While Alec agrees, I try not to think too hard about the fact that Bex talked about being on a lifestyle website. It's not like we're—

Well, I'm planning on having sex with my best friend and my husband is hooking up with hers, so I guess that's a lifestyle thing? I don't know if that makes us swingers or poly or just a generic open marriage, but it's not a traditional marriage, that's for sure. And while I'm okay with not being in a traditional marriage, there's something about labeling it that makes my stomach do this weird flip.

"Did you guys claim the bedroom with the huge bathtub?" I ask, crossing my arms and pretending to be grumpy about it. I'm not, but it's easier than stressing out over labels.

"We thought we'd let you have first crack at the bedrooms this time," Rafael says with a grin. "Since last time we hogged the shower."

"At least you shared it with us *eventually,*" I say, all haughty-like, and then slowly peruse the rooms again.

I end up choosing the one with a nice shower and bathtub, but not anything overly excessive. Bex says the bed is an Alaskan king, which is larger than any bed I've ever seen, except the ones in the other two bedrooms. Since it's their anniversary, they should pick from the two more elaborate rooms. And hopefully we'll all get to use the whirlpool tub and humongous shower, anyway.

"Really?" Bex asks, and I shrug.

"I like the closet in this one. You two claim yours, and then let's meet on the back deck? We brought champagne."

***

After I drop our bags off and Alec pulls the champagne out from his bag, I start to head towards the deck, but Alec grabs my hand and pulls me against him. He presses a soft kiss to my mouth then pulls back a few inches, raising his eyebrows in a silent question.

I nod, then follow up with, "You?" He nods an affirmative and I pull him in for another kiss before leaning back and then giving him a light smack in the ass. "Go out to the deck, I'm going to see if I can find something to drink this in."

Anticipation is coursing through me as I search through the cabinets in the gorgeous, modern kitchen, finally finding four long-stemmed glasses. I hear voices, and through the large windows I can see Bex and Rafael joining Alec outside. Alec seems the least nervous of any of us—Bex is doing the thing where she starts talking at sixty miles an hour about anything and everything, while Rafael is quieter, but clearing his throat and cracking his knuckles.

Alec nods his head towards the door so I head out, working to cover my anxiety with confidence. Plus, Alec and I had discussed how to break the ice, because we suspected this would happen.

The deck is gorgeous, overlooking trees and gentle rolling hills. I place the glasses on a small cocktail table, while Alec hands the bottle over to Rafael.

"You guys do the honors. Happy Anniversary."

"Sixteen down, sixty to go," Rafael says, looking over at Bex, and they share a sweet kiss before Rafael pops the cork.

Champagne goes *everywhere*.

"The hell?" Bex says, and Rafael turns to Alec.

"Did you shake it before giving it to me?"

Alec laughs and shrugs, and Rafael reaches over and shoves him, but he's laughing too.

"My shirt is soaked," says Bex, to which I throw up my hands.

"Should probably take it off, then."

Bex grins at me and rolls her eyes, but in a swift movement has tugged her shirt up over her head. She's wearing shorts and a black lace bra that's largely see-through, and there's a drip running down her neck and over her collarbone. I take a step closer, watching it.

"May I?" I ask quietly, and after studying me for a moment she nods.

Ducking my head I catch that drop with my mouth, then kiss my way up to her ear. Her skin is soft and sweet, and she shudders under my attention. Her hands come to rest on my hips as my cup her jawline and I pull back to look at her.

"Hi," I say quietly.

"Hi," she replies.

My pretense as confidence starts to slip, and suddenly my heart is pounding in my chest. I've just realized that the moment we kiss, there's no going back. Kissing her on a vacation that we've planned for the sole purpose of hooking up means something. Something about our friendship, something about Alec's and my marriage, something about the relationship between the four of us.

But I want to kiss her, and I need to stop overthinking things. Fake it until you make it. So I lean forward and press my mouth to hers.

Her lips soften against mine. A brief kiss, and then a second, and on the third I swipe my tongue along her bottom lip and she opens for me. Brushes her tongue against mine. Sighs softly in a way that makes my body hum in excitement.

Her arms slide around my waist as mine encircles her neck and we tilt our heads to fit together better.

"Darce," she sighs, and I capture her mouth again, running one hand through her hair. I tug on her ponytail holder so that it comes tumbling down in brown waves and lightly scratch her scalp with my fingernails. She groans lightly and I'm already damp between my legs, ready for whatever part of her she'll give me.

I kiss along her jawline, stopping to suck at a pulse point, and her head drops to the side to give me easier access. "Champagne was a good call," she murmurs as one of my hands drifts down to her tits, running a thumb across her hard nipple.

"Apparently," I tease, because she's once again hard enough to cut glass. But I love it, because it keeps me from having to guess, from wondering if she's into what I'm doing or playing along out of pity.

If her nipples are visible through clothing, it's a good sign that she's enjoying herself.

And right now? Her nipples are impossible to ignore. My hand cups the underside of her breast, molding it in the direction of my mouth, and my lips close around her peak. The lace of her bra is rough against my lips and tongue, and when she groans again I want to strip her naked, taste every inch of her.

There's a grunt behind me, and when I pull myself off Bex to look, Alec has pinned Rafael to the wall with his forearm, and they're kissing. Alec's hand is over Rafael's crotch, cupping him through his clothes, and Rafael's already hard.

"Inside?" I ask, and the guys pull apart, panting.

"Yeah," my husband says, not taking his eyes off Rafael.

I grab Bex's hand and tug her through the door, to the bedroom that no one's claimed. Like the other rooms it's large, with hardwood floors and a plush carpet in the center. A couple of armchairs, a dresser with a TV, and a bed that's probably twice the size of Alec's and mine at home.

"Up," I say, pointing at the bed. She laughs but follows my directions, and then I crawl into her lap, straddling her and running my hands through her hair.

Alec and Rafael are next to us, though they're not nearly as gentle with each other. Rafael's straddling Alec's chest, pinning his hands to the bed.

"Same safe word as last time?" Alec asks, and Rafael nods, as do Bex and I. We didn't get particularly kinky on our last vacation, but having a common language made sense, and made sure we were all fully on board. *Yellow* meant stop, and even though no one said it, we all knew that we could, that the word was there if we needed it.

"Good," Alec says, then he grins up at Rafael. One quick-as-a-flash maneuver, and suddenly Rafael is the one on his back, hands held in place by one of Alec's.

"Damn," Bex says under her breath, and Rafael laughs.

The laughs quickly turn back to moans, though, as Alec's free hand undoes Rafael's shorts and Alec shoves his hand in there.

"You going to let me suck this gorgeous cock of yours, or you going to keep fighting me?" he asks.

"You can suck it," Rafael groans.

"Good answer."

"How about you?" I ask, turning my attention back to Bex. "Do I get my mouth on you tonight?"

She nods so I slide off her, standing at the foot of the bed, and pull her towards me. I tug off her shorts and then her underwear, leaning forward to give her breast another nip with my teeth before settling on the floor, her thighs over my shoulders.

Bex has propped herself up on her elbows, and watches me as I press a kiss to her thigh, then nibble at her skin with my teeth. "Haven't done this in a while," I say, trying to sound like I'm joking rather than massively insecure about my oral talents. "So forgive me if I'm out of practice."

"I'm not worried," she says, looking at me seriously. Looking *through* me, because she's my best friend of almost two decades, and knows how to see through my bravado and into the very heart of me.

It's almost too much, this eye contact, so I look at her pussy, pink and wet and...

"Did you get a Brazilian?" I know she hates them, but this is way too smooth to be from shaving.

She flushes and nods. "I know you prefer Alec hairless, so I figured..." Bex shrugs.

For *me*? Damn. I'm a little speechless that she got a wax with me in mind. I'm not sure I deserve something so thoughtful, but I'll do my best to make it worth it.

Thanking her with orgasms seems appropriate.

I start with two fingers, sliding through her slick folds and around her clit. She's so wet for me, and I slip along her skin with no resistance. A soft sigh means I'm doing something right, but I know Bex likes to edge, likes the tension of being about to come but not coming yet, so I'm in no hurry. She can tell, because she's dropped off her elbows, laying flat against the bed, like she's in for the long haul.

More stroking her pussy, approaching but never touching her clit. I kiss along her thighs, sometimes swapping out lips for tongue or teeth, and after a few minutes she starts moving slightly, trying to place her clit along the trail of my fingers.

"Impatient?" I ask, chuckling, and she groans.

"You don't have to make me orgasm this very second, but my clit is screaming for you."

I nip at her knee, removing my hand from her slick folds and skimming my nails lightly along her thighs instead. "Is it?"

She doesn't answer this time, but I do get another groan.

I laugh again, then return my hands to her pussy, holding her open with my thumbs and blowing air against her wet core.

"Fuck!"

"You doing okay there, mi vida?" asks Rafael, though his voice is strangled and tight. Alec's fist is wrapped around him, pumping slowly.

"I think Darcy's trying to kill me," she says.

"Same with Alec," he replies, and Alec laughs, ducking his head to suck one of Rafael's balls into his mouth.

Alec, too, is rewarded with a grunt.

"They complain a lot," I tell my husband, and he dramatically rolls his eyes and nods.

"It's not like we're not going to let them come!"

"Eventually," I add, then quickly flick a tongue against Bex's clit and she yelps and jolts.

"Did you two become sadists since we last did this?" she asks.

"Whatever. You know you love it," I reply, and take her lack of a response as proof that I'm right.

So I lick her again, but this time it's slow, savoring her feel and taste and her hot skin against the slide of my tongue. She sighs, and I do it again, and again, and again, turned on a little more every time she makes a noise that signals her pleasure.

Alec, too, has given Rafael his mouth. First it's just his lips wrapped around the head, but as my tongue speeds up its movements, so does Alec's mouth, going deeper and deeper on Rafael's cock. We're both speeding up, going faster and deeper, and then Alec and I make eye contact, and when he winks at me I know exactly what he's suggesting. I nod, and then we both come to an immediate stop, pulling away.

"You fucking asshole!" groans Rafael, while Bex whines, "Oh come on!"

I burst into giggles, and this is my favorite kind of sex. The kind where you laugh and call each other names and tease each other and just have fun. And that we're having it with Bex and Rafael is still a little mind blowing.

I give Alec a nod and he nods back and then our mouths are on them again, keeping the pace we were going when we stopped. As we continue, Bex's hands grasp at the comforter and Rafael fists Alec's hair. I slide a finger into Bex's pussy, and then a second, trying to feel around for the spot that I discovered last time around. Rougher, but spongy when I prod it, and I can tell that I'm there when Bex gasps.

Alec pulls his mouth off Rafael, continuing to work him over with his hand while he sucks on his balls. Then, releasing with a wet *pop*, he glances over at me. "We going to try to time them?"

"Don't think we're quite at that level yet," I reply, but start sucking on Bex's clit, because I know that'll get her there faster.

"Right, which is why I said *try*."

I nod against Bex, and Alec grins, replacing his hand with his mouth once again. He works Rafael's cock quick and deep, and I remember how much of a turn-on it is to watch my husband go down on a dude.

Rafael's free hand reaches out for Bex. He grabs her wrist, and she lets go of the comforter to thread her fingers with his, and I can tell that they're both squeezing because of how white their knuckles are.

I'm trying to take my cues from both of them, hoping for a simultaneous orgasm. Sucking her clit, rubbing her g-spot with my fingers, and—because I know she likes it a little rough—scraping the nails of my free hand along her thigh, just a touch more than gentle.

"I'm gonna," she gasps, and then her thighs squeeze my head as her back arches. She's whimpering and her pussy shudders around my fingers. I don't stop, continuing until she says that's it's enough, that it's too much, that she's done now. And only then do I pull away, withdrawing my fingers and wiping my mouth with the back of my hand. I press quick kisses up her body as I crawl up to her, settling next to her, and she gives me a quick kiss.

Alec and Rafael finish a minute later, with Rafael warning him and Alec ignoring the warning, swallowing down his release as he tugs on Rafael's balls. My body responds as I watch them, pussy clenching and mouth watering as Rafael groans, squeezing Bex's hand as he comes. Then Rafael lies limp against the bed as Alec flops down next to him.

"Damn, didn't time it right," Alec says.

"Guess you'll have to try again," Rafael replies, smirking as Alec props himself up on his elbow and shoves Rafael's shoulder. Rafael pulls him down for a kiss, and then a second.

"Happy anniversary," I say, stretching out next to Bex, and she grins over at me. And it's so weird that it's the same grin I remember from move-in day freshman year of college, when she introduced herself as my roommate, except she's doing it naked and the taste of her is still on my lips.

"We thought it might be kind of weird to invite you on our anniversary trip, of all times. But we were already planning on being kid-free, so it seemed like the timing made sense."

"Plus, we both just got to come without doing any work," Rafael says. "Pretty decent anniversary gift. Was that the plan the whole time? Douse us in champagne and then lick it off?"

"We thought it might cut the awkwardness," I say. "Plus last time you guys made the first move, so we figured it was our turn."

"Brilliant," Bex says, scooting closer to her husband and then reaching out to tug me so that I'm snug up against her as well. "Give me a minute to recover and then we can figure out what's for dinner."

"No rush," I say, leaning over to nip at her earlobe. "I already ate."

Chapter 7

THE GROCERIES WE BROUGHT include some things for more labor-intensive dinners, but we default to salad and a frozen pizza for tonight. We'll save the fancy stuff for a day where we have more time and we're motivated to put in some real effort.

Afterwards we stretch out in the living room. Bex's head is in my lap and I stroke her hair lazily while her feet get massaged by Rafael. It's a pretty cushy spot, but I don't mind, because it means I get to touch her. And there were days and nights over the past six months where all I wanted to do was touch her.

"So is the plan sex all week, or are we going to do other things to break the orgasms up?" Alec asks from his spot the cushy leather recliner.

"There are some nice hiking trails around here," Rafael offers. "And a swimming hole on the property."

"Skinny dipping?" Alec asks, and I reach over to punch him lightly.

"I thought you wanted to break up the orgasms a bit?"

"We'll break it up with the hike there and the hike back," he says with a wink and I laugh.

"Winery tour?" Bex suggests, and I nod enthusiastically.

"Yes! And then we can have drunk sex, since it doesn't work with the guys."

"It doesn't?" Rafael asks, and Bex and I exchange a look because I've told her before that Alec struggles to get it up when he's drunk. I'd forgotten that Rafael doesn't have that issue.

"Not everyone's a stallion like you are, babe," she says to her husband, and Alec throws me a dirty look.

"It happens to a lot of guys," he says.

"I'm just teasing!" I place a pillow under Bex's head and move to the recliner, settling on Alec's lap. "I love you, even when you're limp."

He mimics me talking with an exaggerated head shake, but wraps his arms around my waist and nibbles at my neck. I tease him because I know he can take it.

"Yeah, yeah, yeah," he says. "You'll owe me for that later."

Bex rolls to her stomach, now facing us. "Not later, now! She should owe you now!"

"Bex has gotten pretty horny," Alec says to me in an exaggerated whisper, and I laugh.

"She's always been horny."

"She just didn't tell you about it," Rafael adds, reaching over to give her ass a gentle smack.

"So is Darcy giving you a blowjob or not?" Bex asks expectantly.

Alec looks at me and grins. "Later. Maybe I'll make you guys listen to it through the wall."

Last year that's how the whole thing got started—it turns out we're all into eavesdropping on other people having sex. And then one thing led to another and...

"Listening to each other through the wall is *so* last time," Bex says.

"Speaking of which," Rafael says. "When did you figure out the walls were so thin? Did you know the first time you had sex, or was it when we got it on that you realized?"

Alec and I exchange a glance, and he answers. "Halfway through the first night. Some noise came from your room, and then you were whispering, and that's when we realized you could hear everything."

"And you kept having sex?" Rafael asks, and I shrug.

"We figured if you wanted us to stop you'd have banged on the wall or something. Granted, we didn't realize it would end up like *this*."

I gesture at the four of us, in various states of undress. I don't think any of us could have guessed at the beginning of the last trip that we'd end up... swinging or whatever. But we're here, and if earlier today was any indication, we're not interested in stopping anytime soon.

"And then Alec fingerbanged you in the ocean," Rafael says, and I sit up straight at that, looking at them, because I didn't know they'd picked up on that.

"How'd you know about *that*?"

"You weren't subtle, like, at all," Bex says, giggling. "And it was right after I gave Rafe a hand job in the ocean."

Alec makes a strangled sound. "We missed that? How did we miss that?"

I wave my hand dismissively. "Enough about last year. New memories and orgasms this year."

"Starting with the blow job you owe Alec," Bex says, and Rafael growls, giving her backside another love tap.

"Stop thinking about someone else's dick when mine is right here," he says, and Bex wiggles her eyebrows.

"Does it help if I'm thinking about his abs instead of his dick?"

I pull his shirt up, showing off said abs to the room. "These?"

She fans herself and Rafael reaches over to haul her into his lap. "Maybe you'll owe me, too," he says.

Bex feigns looking upset. "Oh, no, will I have to go down on you? Anything but that."

He grins. "You know if you want to go down on me, you just have to ask. You don't have to make me jealous."

She laughs and kisses him, then looks over at us.

"So what are the sleeping arrangements tonight? Together? Apart? Which room?"

"Together in the third room?" I offer. "That way if it starts feeling too crowded for anyone they can go back to their room without it being weird."

Rafael nods, lifting Bex up and placing her gently on her feet. "Shall we go to bed?"

I nod, sliding off Alec and then reach out my hands, tugging him to standing. "We shall."

Chapter 8

LIKE MOST OF MY packing dilemmas, I spent *way* too much time trying to figure out what to bring to sleep in. Bex has that natural, girl next door kind of gorgeousness that means she can sleep in one of Rafael's shirts and look fuckable in the morning, but some of us have to work a little harder. At home I default to a negligee or a lacy shorts and top number, but I wasn't sure if next to everyone else I'd just look overdressed for bed. So of course I ended up bringing multiple options, and Alec commented how my bag was *bigger* than last time even though we were spending *less* time there.

I'd blamed it on the toys.

But tonight no one even stops over at their luggage before going to the third bedroom to start shedding clothing. The guys strip down to their boxers, and—as predicted—Bex grabs the shirt Rafael peeled off and pulls it on. I duck into our bedroom, and pick my lowest maintenance choice—an oversized tank top that shows off a good amount of sideboob.

When I return Alec makes a big show of pulling the armhole away from my body, checking my tits out, and then pulling me close.

"If I told you that you had a nice body, would you hold it against me?" he whispers in my ear.

I pull away a few inches, laughing. "Pretty sure you've done that one before. You're losing your touch."

He winks and then whispers again, "You're gorgeous," before giving me a gentle shove towards the bed.

Falling back dramatically, I crawl between the sheets, hoping my flush isn't obvious. Alec has a knack for knowing when I'm feeling insecure, for saying the perfect thing to help even when I've tried to keep it under wraps. For knowing when I need a reminder that even after all these years, he's still ridiculously attracted to me.

Bex meets me in the middle of the bed, immediately stretching out into a starfish position. "Oh my God this bed is *amazing*. Rafe, come check it out."

I wedge my shoulder against hers, shoving a little bit. "Move over, you're hogging the whole thing!"

"It's a double king, which I didn't even know was a thing," she says, refusing to move. "So there's no way I'm taking up all of it."

I reach over to squeeze her side, and Bex immediately dissolves into giggles.

"Tickles!" she gasps, reaching out for me, and next thing I know we're two women in our late 30s having an honest to goodness tickle fight until we're exhausted, tears streaming down our faces from laughing so hard.

Alec has stretched out on the bed, propping himself up on one elbow. "I think next on the agenda was a tickle fight? Am I remembering correctly, Rafael?"

Rafael nods and grins, licking his lips suggestively. Honestly, second to getting to hook up with Bex, my favorite part of this whole arrangement is seeing this side of him that I never knew firsthand. Alec makes dirty jokes every chance he gets, and Bex and I have talked about sex since college, but the only thing I knew about Rafael was what Bex told me. Now I get to see him be fun and flirty and playful in bed.

One of the lines Bex and I didn't cross last time was sharing each others' husbands. Alec and Bex didn't get it on with each other, and neither did Rafael and I. And that's not something I'm looking to do on this trip either—for one, I get dick fifty-one weeks out of the year, this is my chance for pussy.

Second, sharing Alec with Rafael is hard enough. I don't want to share him with my best friend.

It's not that I don't trust him, or don't trust her, because I do. Implicitly. But that's not something I really want to experiment with right now, no matter how hot Rafael is.

And he is pretty damn sexy. Bex did a good job picking a husband.

"Like you didn't just get to watch Darcy go down on me," Bex says.

"I was slightly distracted by this hunk over here," Rafael says, gesturing towards Alec. "Besides, she got you off, shouldn't you return the favor?"

Turns out we're all a bit exhibitionist, and a bit voyeur. There's just something super alluring about knowing people are getting hot and bothered from seeing me get off. I guess I could have figured out the voyeurism thing because I like porn, but live? It's even better. And watching my husband with Rafael is also way hotter than I ever could have guessed–I love seeing how that side of him is a little different from what it is with me.

Bex rolls her eyes, but I shrug. "I mean, your husband has a point."

"I guess. If I *have* to," Bex says, then leans over to close the gap between us.

The kiss is soft, sweet, and she slides her hand down to my ass, pulling me closer. We're touching from our head to our toes, our breasts pressed against each other, and I hook my leg over her hip. Her hand lands on the skin of my thigh, gently stroking up and down, from ass to knee, and for a while we just kiss.

Then our hands start wandering a bit more. I cup her breasts, running my thumb along her hard nipples, and she pulls me closer, encouraging me to grind against her leg. I don't need to be told twice, rubbing myself against her as her lips move from mine to my neck, then teeth graze my earlobe. With my mouth free I vocalize more, sighing and moaning and whispering encouragement.

When her hands settle at my hips, hooking under the waistband of my underwear, I shift so that she can tug them off, and reach for hers.

"This is supposed to be about you," she says, lifting her mouth from my skin. But even though I've just had her, I still want more.

"What if we take care of each other?"

There's only a moment's hesitation before she nods, shifting her hips up off the bed so that I can pull her underwear down her legs, and then we take off our shirts and we're naked.

Opening ourselves up for each other, my hand drifts from her hip to between her legs, where she's wet and soft and waiting for me. Her movements mirror mine, and an involuntary shudder goes through my body.

"Good?" she asks, and I nod before leaning forward to kiss her again, sliding my fingers through her folds until I find the nub of her clit.

It's a little slow and lazy at first, reminding ourselves what the other one likes, how to evoke the sighs and moans that we both love to hear. But soon we develop a rhythm, breath and hands moving faster, in tandem with each other. Her fingers slide inside me and I moan, throwing my head back as she searches for my G-spot, and I do the same, finding where she's a little more swollen and a lot more responsive.

Then I tuck my forehead against her shoulder, eyes closed as I try to focus on both giving and receiving pleasure, on the back and forth of it. "Darce," she whimpers, and I love the way she says it, like it's too much effort to say my whole name, like she's too overcome.

"You close?" I ask, and I feel her nod. "Me too."

Our hands are flying now, our breaths coming in short gasps as we chase release. "I'm gonna," she moans, and I turn my head to scrape my teeth along her neck, a gentle love bite to give her the brief sting I learned she sometimes needs to orgasm. And it was well timed because she stiffens, arching against the bed with a cry.

Somehow her hand is still going, some subconscious urge to help me reach my peak even when she's mid-orgasm. And I'm close, panting and saying things I won't be able to remember, a combination of 'yes' and 'fuck' and 'right there' and 'Bex.' A moment later the tightness that has built up in my pussy releases with a jolt to all my nerve endings and I join her in bliss. "Bex!" I yelp. "Goddammit, that's– *fuck*."

Then we're limp against the bed, breathing hard and covered with a light sheen of sweat. And so fucking satiated, so fucking relaxed, so fucking blissed out.

The guys, it seems, have started their own round. Rafael is on top of Alec, pinning Alec's hands above his head with one hand, and gripping both their cocks with the other. I know Alec, know he could wrestle himself out of Rafael's grasp if he wanted to, but he doesn't appear to have any interest in doing that, eyes locked on Rafael's.

"You're going to fucking come for me," Rafael growls in low tones. "You're going to come all over your stomach, and you're going to be covered in cum, and you can't fucking wait, can you."

"I can't," Alec gasps.

I've known that before we were married, when Alec dated guys and girls, he was a fan of both fucking and being fucked. When it's both of us he's usually the one in charge, and even on the rare occasions I take charge, I've never seen this side of him. It's a little disorienting, and I try to ignore the voice in the back of my head that wonders if this is something he's missing in our marriage, if he wants me to take more of a lead sometimes.

Rafael is pumping both of their cocks at once, and every time his hand flexes in a squeeze Alec arches up towards him, breath hitching.

"Just do it already," Alec groans, and Rafael grins down at him.

"Do what?" he asks, pumping his hand a little faster. "This?"

Alec nods, chest heaving with the effort of his breathing, and Rafael speeds up a little more, and then a little more. I recognize the gasps that are escaping Alec, his sign that he's about to come, and then Rafael stops suddenly and Alec groans loud enough that I'm surprised the walls don't vibrate.

"Stop teasing him!" Bex says, the grin in her voice evident even though her back is to me. I slide behind her, pressing my breasts up against her back and wrapping my arm around her waist.

"Yeah, listen to your wife," Alec croaks.

"Hush, you," Rafael says at Bex, though when he looks at her there's undisguised affection in his eyes. Then he glances down at Alec. "What's the magic word?" he taunts.

"Please?" Alec's chest is still heaving. "Please let me come?"

Rafael nods, then his hand starts moving again, pace steady. Alec reaches up and wraps his hand around the back of Rafael's neck, pulling him closer and crushing their mouths together. They kiss as Rafael keeps jerking them off, a punishing, bruising kiss rather than anything gentle or sweet. It's like Alec's fighting for control of Rafael's mouth, since Rafael is in charge of everything else. He sucks Rafael's lower lip into his mouth and Rafael groans as Alec's hips start thrusting up towards him, contributing to the effort.

Rafael pulls his mouth away. "I'm gonna," he warns, and Alec nods.

"Fuck yes you are. I am too, we're both going to." Even though he's underneath Rafael, even though Rafael is the one with dicks in hand, somehow Alec has taken back control, his hand running through Rafael's hair and fisting it. "Do it."

Rafael does, all jerky movements and quiet groans, and then a moment later Alec does too, louder and frozen with his back arched and ass fully lifted off the bed.

A few moments later he collapses back and Rafael drops on top of him, burying his face in Alec's neck. "You're making a mess," Alec says with a laugh, and Rafael rolls off him.

I get up to grab a washcloth from the bathroom, and Bex joins me, pressing a kiss to my bare shoulder and glancing at my reflection in the mirror as I wet the towel and give it to her, then a second.

"You okay? You were quiet in there."

"Just watching," I say, even though that's not entirely true. I'm trying to sort out how I feel about Alec seeming to enjoy being dominated in bed. Having someone he can wrestle for control with.

Bex knows me, knows there's something just a tiny bit off, but also knows well enough not to push, at least not right now. I press a quick kiss to her mouth and thread my fingers with hers, tugging for her to follow me, and we wordlessly wipe off their stomachs.

As I sweep the damp washcloth along Alec's abs he reaches up to catch a lock of hair between his thumb and forefinger, tweaking it gently. His eyes are closed when I glance over at him, a peaceful look on his face, a half-smile on his lips. I press my mouth against his, and the half-smile turns to a full one.

"Love you," I whisper, and when he whispers it back I feel a bit better, a bit more secure.

I take my and Bex's washcloths back to the bathroom, rinsing them off and hanging them on the towel rack to dry, then look at myself in the mirror. I didn't expect to find it so difficult to share Alec this time around. Last time it seemed easy enough—Bex was a little hesitant, and I was the one talking her down. But something about this time, about how we set everything up, something feels different. Not enough to stop, but having to wrap my mind around it this time is bringing up something new.

It might be that I'm not the only one doing this intentionally; Alec is too. Bex gives me something that Alec doesn't, and I love that, but Rafael is giving Alec something I'm not, which feels harder. Weirder. I *want* to be able to give him everything he needs, even when I don't expect him to do the same for me.

I wonder if I'm the only one feeling this way.

When I go back in the room everyone is situated under the covers, a space near the middle of the bed for me between Bex and Alec. Between two of my favorite people, the two people on the planet who know me better than pretty much anyone. The guys are discussing basketball and Bex is on her phone and it looks so comfortable and *normal*, even, that I'm again confused where my hesitation is coming from. Because the three people I trust most in the world are right here, in this room.

I join them in bed, resting my chin on Bex's shoulder, my arm draped across her stomach as she scrolls TikTok. "Somehow I ended up on KinkTok," she admits.

"Somehow?" I say, and she laughs and shrugs.

"Because the TikTok algorithm is all-seeing and all-knowing. And possibly also a little bit because I watched a video of a really hot guy saying *good girl* like twenty five times."

"Until I made her stop," Rafael says.

"And then he started saying it to me and I nearly had a spontaneous orgasm," Bex adds.

"Mmmmm. I need to learn how to have a spontaneous orgasm," I say.

Alec leans over, using a sexy whisper voice right in my ear. "You're *my* good girl."

My pussy tingles, and I turn my head to look at him, nodding. "Not bad, hot stuff."

"No more sex tonight!" Bex insists, batting away Rafael's hands where they're drifting over her breasts. "Save it for tomorrow, horndog."

"Look who's calling who a horndog," he replies, though he does stop, settling under the covers.

Alec leans over to turn off the lamp that's on the nightstand on his side of the bed, then settles next to me, wrapping an arm around my waist and hauling my back against his chest. One knee nudges between mine, and I relax against him.

"Sweet dreams," says Bex through the quiet of the room.

Wrapped in Alec's arms, pressed against his chest, my nerves are settled again. Because he's Alec, and we're committed to each other, and nothing that happens this trip can change that.

I reach over and thread my fingers with hers. "How could I have anything but?"

Chapter 9

THE NEXT MORNING, AFTER a pancake breakfast, we change into our swimsuits, hike-appropriate athleisure over it. Even though it's only ten by the time we head out, it's sweltering, and we're all sweating and sticky by the time we reach the swimming hole.

The spot we read about is small, shaded by towering cypress trees, one of which has a rope swing attached. The far side is a gentle slope, and the rocky shore ends with a large rock wall that forms a natural cliff. But the side we've arrived on has a sharp drop off, and by the time Bex and I have shimmied out of our coverups the guys have already shed their shirts and jumped into the deep water, splashing us with a little too much glee. The water is fed by underwater springs, and it's apparently the same cool temperature year round.

"Give me a minute!" I yelp as the cold water hits my skin.

"You just need to jump in," says Rafael. "Rip the band aid off."

Bex does, and when she surfaces she's grinning, treading water as she looks over at me. "Come on Darcy," she says, and I dip a toe in and then recoil.

"It's freezing!" I whine, and this time Bex joins in on splashing me, and I back away from the bank as the droplets hit my skin.

"It's not that bad once you're in it!" promises Bex, but when I hesitate a little more, Alec and Rafael exchange a look and then get out of the water, stalking towards me.

"What are you doing?" I squeal, as Alec hoists me over his shoulder and heads to where the rope swing is. He grabs my hands and Rafael my feet.

"One," they call out in unison, swinging me towards the water. "Two... and three!"

When they let go I fly through the air a short distance, pinching my nose shut before I hit the water, laughing and spluttering as I surface.

"I hate you!" I tease, though they're right, it actually feels pretty nice once your whole body has been submerged.

"No you don't," says Alec, who's jumped back in himself and is swimming towards me.

"I do!" I argue, and he wraps his arm around my waist, dragging me to the shallow part of the far bank and pressing me against the rock wall that lines that side of the swimming hole.

"You don't," he counters, looking at Rafael and nodding him over. "Hold her hands down."

I squirm as if I'm going to fight even though I don't want to, not really. Rafael stands off to the side, pinning my hands above my head on the smooth surface of the rock. Alec hooks his fingers under my bottoms, sliding them down, and I continue wiggling until he covers my pussy with his mouth.

"Fuck," I gasp, my head dropping lightly to the rock behind me, and it's a good thing Rafael has my hands pinned, because my knees go weak at what Alec's doing.

Bex joins us, tugging my suit so that one tit is exposed, and I'm geared up, waiting for the warm wetness of her mouth to envelop me, when instead she drips some of the chilly water on my nipple.

I shudder, arching towards her as one foot lifts from the ground, curling up by its own accord. "Bex," I gasp.

She smirks at me. "Hmmm?"

If I had a hand free I'd fist it into her hair, guiding her to my exposed skin, but they're held down by Rafe. And Alec takes my hips in his hands, pressing my lower half against the smooth surface, leaving me with no space to wiggle.

"Please," I pant, as Alec laps at my clit.

"Please what?" she asks, happy at having the upper hand.

"Put your mouth on me!"

She laughs, pressing a kiss to the top of my breast, and then another and then another. The kisses get sloppier as they approach my nipple, and she pauses occasionally to lightly suck on a patch of skin or graze her teeth against me, but she avoids the sensitive tip.

I glance up at Rafael who's watching intently. "She's mean," I whimper, and he nods, amused.

"Put her out of her misery, mi vida," he says playfully to Bex, who grins and finally, *finally* covers me with her mouth.

Her tongue sweeps around my nipple slowly as Alec's on my clit isswifter, and I feel so fucking spoiled, having these two mouths work me over until my heart is pounding and my breath is noisy.

"I'm jealous," Rafael admits, and I realize that even though we haven't gotten it on with each other, we still have this bond because we share the same partners. It could just as easily be him here, pinned against this rock as Bex sucks his dick and Alec eats his ass. Though I'd probably get distracted enough watching that he'd be able to wiggle free—right now I have neither the interest, nor the ability, to escape.

"It's really good," I whimper, and he grins at me.

"I can tell."

Alec has taken the foot that was pressed against the rock and hooked that leg over his shoulder, and now he's driving his fingers into me, curling up against my g-spot. And I'm close, right there, on the edge, trying to hold the pleasure off so that I can feel this forever, when Rafael leans over and I feel his hot breath against my ear.

"Come for them," he whispers.

And I do.

***

"If anyone was within earshot they should be showing up any moment now wondering what the hell that was," Bex says after I'm mostly recovered, sitting in Alec's lap in the shallow water.

"I can't help it if I'm enthusiastic when I come," I say, tossing my hair over my shoulder.

Rafe laughs. "There's enthusiastic, and then there's that," he says.

"Loud," Alec clarifies, nuzzling my neck. "You're loud."

"What do you guys do at home?" Bex asks. "You obviously can't do that when the kids are sleeping down the hall."

"It helps that we're on the other side of the house," I say. "That, plus music, plus Herculean efforts to hold it in all make it so that they've never mentioned it. Hopefully we're not scarring them for life."

"Herculean efforts," Bex snorts.

"We're not all gifted with the silent orgasm like you are!"

"Bex has her own tells," Rafael says, reaching over to rub a thumb across the pebbled nipple that's visible through the top of her suit, and her eyes flutter shut. When he pulls his hand away she crawls over to him, slipping into his lap and pulling his arms around her as she relaxes against him.

"It's a blessing and a curse," she admits. "It means Rafe knows when I'm turned on, but it means *everyone* knows when I'm turned on. Well, everyone who pays attention, at least."

"I pay attention," I say with a grin, and she laughs.

"Well *now* you do."

"Yeah, definitely a new thing. Totally didn't notice in college."

"Darcy!" she exclaims, splashing water in my direction. "When did you first notice it?"

"Sophomore year, I think? I walked in on a make out session, and the headlights were on, didn't go away until like fifteen minutes after he left."

Bex covers her face with her hands. "I can't believe you've been paying attention to my nipples for so long!"

"Well I wasn't really thinking about hooking up with you then, but I've always thought you've had fantastic tits."

Rafael moves his hands up to cover them, pressing a kiss to the spot where her neck meets her shoulder. "That she does."

Chapter 10

Later that afternoon, while the guys take turns at the grill preparing our steak dinner, Bex and I stretch out on the hammock together, head to foot.

"Question," she says as she drapes an arm across my shins.

"Answer."

"Okay, but you can't get excited or make it a big thing."

Pushing myself up a bit so that I can see her better I grin. "Oh?"

"I said not to make it a big deal!" she complains, flushing pink, which only makes me more curious.

"You knew that the only possible response to that was me making it a big thing. Also, are you blushing?"

"No!" she says, turning pinker.

"You are! Okay, now you *have* to tell me."

She gives an exasperated sigh. "Anal."

"Ooooh!" I switch my head and feet and turn to face her. "What about it?"

"I think I want to try it?" Her voice is interested, but hesitant, and I can tell by the way she's not quite meeting my gaze that she's shy about asking.

"Yeah? And Rafael?"

"We've talked about it. But we've never really tried it. Or anything in the butt. And I'm afraid of it hurting."

"The trick is prep and lube. Here, come with me."

Taking her hand I slide off the hammock and tug for her to follow. "Be right back!" I call to the guys and head inside, to my and Alec's room and the bag of toys we brought.

"Oh my God, did you order the whole catalog?" she asks, and I roll my eyes.

"Whatever, I know you guys have a collection of your own."

"It's not this... diverse, though," she says, pawing through vibrators, dildos, nipple clamps, cock rings, and more. She holds up a black silicone toy and I nod.

"Perfect, that's one that I was looking for. Butt plug with a prostate massager, for Rafael if he wants it. Assuming he's into butt play too."

"He is. I think."

"You haven't talked about it?"

Bex shakes her head. "I don't know. We just haven't."

I give her an amused look. "You talked about whether to invite us on your anniversary, but putting things in his ass, that's a bridge too far."

She rolls her eyes, but she's grinning. "Whatever. We will! I just wanted advice from you first."

"Well..." I produce the small, bright pink butt plug. "This is how I say you start. Lube up good, play with this. Maybe have sex with it in. Same with the one for Rafael. Just try it, see if it does anything for you. If it does, you can use a bigger one, work your way up to sex. No anal sex tonight, just anal play."

"Okay," she says, staring at the butt plug like it's going to come to life and bite her, and I shake my head softly and lean forward to give her a quick kiss.

"There's nothing to be nervous about, I promise. We always clean them after so they're good, take them. You have lube? Cleaning stuff?"

She nods.

"And your bathroom has a bidet, right? Do you know how to use it?"

She nods again, head movements jerkier this time, and eyes widening. I do my best not to laugh at her response because I know she's nervous, but damn, it's adorable.

"That's probably plenty as far as *prep* prep. And that's it."

"Okay," she says slowly, taking both the pink one for her and the black one for Rafael.

"Perfect. You'll have fun tonight! We'll do separate bedrooms so you guys can have some privacy."

"We don't have to do it ton−" she starts, but I press my lips together and shake my head.

"It's fine. This week is about sexual experimentation, but it doesn't always have to be together. Plus, you've got that gorgeous bath tub, so if you're worried about soreness you can sit in there afterwards. And you guys exploring butt play is hot, I want to hear all about it tomorrow."

She blushes, nodding again, and this time my affection for her and how cute and shy she is bubbles over into a friendly laugh. Leaning forward I give her another kiss, and this one lingers as I slip my hand around the back of her neck. She opens her mouth for me, and our tongues brush.

Alec's voice from the doorway startles me. "You guys playing without us?"

Pulling apart I shake my head, grinning at him. "Just lending Bex some of our toys. They might try something new tonight."

When Bex holds up the plugs, Alec's eyebrows raise, and then heat darkens his eyes.

"You guys are doing that tonight?" he asks.

"Maybe," Bex says. "I need to talk to Rafe first."

Alec licks his lips. "Nice."

"So you're stuck with me," I say, and he reaches his hand out, tugging me towards him. He gives my ass a squeeze with both hands.

"And what am I supposed to do with you?"

I shrug with one shoulder, giving him a coy smile. "I'm sure you can come up with something."

Laughing against my mouth, he nods and gives me a kiss.

***

Before dinner Bex pulls Rafael away, and when they come back they're all giggles and stolen glances. Bex picks at her steak and salad, and she and Rafael can't keep their eyes off each other. Her hand sneaks under the table a handful of times, as does his, followed by loud swallows and heated looks. It's like the beginning of their relationship, when they were going at it like rabbits and anytime they surfaced to grace their friends with their presence they were almost nauseating to be around.

Now I find it cute, though. Sixteen years married and they still get nervous and bubbly around each other.

"I have butterflies," she confesses to me as we clear the table. "I don't know when the last time I had butterflies was. Well, present company excluded, of course."

I nod because yes, last year was full of butterflies. But now that she mentions it, I'm not sure when the last time I had butterflies with Alec was. When you've been together for fifteen years, married for a little over thirteen, you get comfortable together. And while that's a wonderful thing, I think I miss the butterflies. The first kisses, the trying something new, the taking a risk with each other and hoping it pays off. Our sex life is active and fulfilling and we mix things up with where and how we do it, but it feels like at this point we've pretty much done it all. We've even had an orgy with our best friends, what's left?

After dinner's cleaned up, Rafael and Bex hover by the door leading to their bedroom. "Are you sure it's okay?" he asks, glancing between Alec and I. I nod, waving them away.

"Of course! Just be loud, so that we can listen in later. And let us know how the bathtub is."

Bex flushes and giggles again before tugging Rafael into their bedroom and closing the door behind them. Then Alec and I settle on the couch, his head in my lap as he clicks through the streaming services to see if there's anything we want to watch.

"Do you miss butterflies?" I ask, my hand stroking his hair idly, and he looks up at me.

"You want to go to San Antonio for the monarch migration? The kids might love that, actually."

I laugh. "No, not those butterflies. New relationship butterflies. Or trying new things butterflies. Like Rafael and Bex tonight."

"Oh." His forehead wrinkles in thought. "I don't know that I've given it much thought, to be honest. I like what we have, what we do. I don't know that anything's necessarily missing."

"I don't either, it's just..." I pause, as I try to figure out how to put into words what I'm feeling. "Maybe part of it is that it's weird to still be experiencing new things and getting the butterflies, but with Bex, instead of with you. And I'm sure you're having some of the same," I add, thinking about how aggressive Rafael and him got, how that's nothing we've ever done together. Nor do I think we necessarily could, because I get the sense the struggle was part of what he was into, but we're not nearly as matched in size. "And that's fine and good, but I also miss feeling it with you. I think I got a little jealous of Bex and Rafael, seeing them tonight."

He pushes up to sit and pulls me into his lap so that I'm straddling him. Hands on my hips, forearms resting along my thighs, his thumb strokes the skin right above my waistband, and I lean into his touch. "Do you want to try something new, then?"

"I don't think it's necessarily that we have to try something new, just that... I don't know."

"You just miss the butterflies," he says.

"I just miss the butterflies," I agree, relieved that he seems to get it.

"So what is it that brings them on?"

"I'm not sure. Maybe anticipation? A little risk, a little uncertainty? Knowing it's going to happen, even if it's inevitable, but not knowing how it's going to end up?"

"Poor you, knowing that every time we have sex it's going to be amazing. No uncertainty there," he teases and I shove him lightly, but I'm grinning.

"I guess it could be worse," I admit. "At least the certainty I'm dealing with is mind-blowing, not mediocre."

"Exactly," he says. "Even *bad* sex with you is stunning."

"Pffft!" I give him another shove. "You've never had bad sex with me."

"True, true," he says, then wraps his arms around my waist and picks me up a little, depositing me on my back on the couch and settling between my legs. "We doing it out here, or going into the bedroom?"

"Romantic way of propositioning me," I say, and he grins, rubbing his quickly hardening cock against me.

"Who needs romance when I have *this*?" he says, shifting against me again. But then he pulls away from me and stands up, holding one hand out and giving a deep bow. "May I have the honor of this fuck?"

I laugh, but put my hand in his. "Yeah, sure."

Chapter 11

ALEC PULLS ME TO standing, then tugs me in the direction of the room we've shared with Bex and Rafael the last few nights. When we get there, though, he holds up one finger to ask me to wait, and disappears for a moment, returning with a blindfold. We've used them before, but it's been a while.

"What's that for?" I ask, and he grins.

"Butterflies."

"I didn't mean–" I start, but he puts a finger against my lips to silence me.

"No talking," he says, then holds up the blindfold. "Can I?"

When I open my mouth to answer he raises his eyebrows, so I close it and nod. He slips the blindfold over my eyes, and the world goes dark.

I wait a moment, and then another, and a minute ticks by without him saying anything. I'm unable to hear any hint of where in the room he might be, and I wonder if he's left, ducked back into the room with our luggage for a toy or something. Then I feel hands on my waist, a tug on the hem of my shirt, and it goes up and over my head. I'm divested of my shorts just as efficiently–they slide down my legs and he helps me step out of them.

My sense of him disappears again, and I can't tell where he is or what he's doing. I'm wearing a matching lacy bra and panties set and do my best to look cute, one hand on my hip that's jutting out, swiping my hair over my opposite shoulder. Is he looking at me? Are his eyes darkening with lust, is he tenting his pants? Or has he shucked off his clothes completely, taken himself in hand? I have an image of him doing that in my mind's eye and imagine his cock, dusky and weeping. Imagine him watching me as he strokes himself with slow lazy pulls as his cock lengthens and thickens.

Just the idea of it is getting me hot and bothered, and I squeeze my thighs together, feeling my breaths quicken. Can he tell that just fantasizing about him is turning me on? Can he see my pulse hammering in my throat as I try to figure out what's next?

Then I hear something, though I can't figure out what, and a moment later his chest is at my back. A dusting of hair brushes against my shoulder blades, so his shirt is off. "I'm going to lead you to bed now," he says quietly in my ear, and I nod, not sure if I'm allowed to talk yet.

He guides me along the floor, and I know that we're getting close because my feet move from the smooth, cool hardwood to the plush area rug that's under the bed. My knee brushes against the comforter and his hand slides across the front of my thigh, pulling my leg up so that I'm kneeling on the bed. Then he bends me forward gently, positioning me on all fours. His fingers hook under the waistband of my underwear and he slides them down my thighs, then helps me remove them completely, and then does the same with my bra.

Then I'm alone again, and the position I'm in has me on display, ass in the air, tits hanging down. Moisture begins to pool between my legs and then I feel gentle hands between my thighs, pulling my legs apart slightly, so that my knees are separate. He's probably just waiting to see how wet I get without him even touching me, waiting to see if my folds start to glisten as my body readies itself for him–his fingers, his mouth, his cock. Whichever part of him I get will let him in easily, will let him slide in with no resistance. And I want them, want him inside me. He can have his pick of where, but the anticipation is killing me as I strain my ears for a hint of anything.

I think I feel warm breath against my pussy and I bite my bottom lip to keep from whimpering. I'm much more likely to get his tongue if he doesn't know I can tell that he's there, if he doesn't think I'm anticipating the warm wet slide of his lips on me.

But then I feel something against my right nipple, which pebbles instantly. I think it's the rough tip of a calloused finger, and then maybe that's the scruff of his five-o-clock shadow against my left nipple, and my chest presses forward, seeking more contact, more friction. He chuckles and I whip my head in the direction of the sound, trying to place his exact location. Soft lips brush against my forehead, between my eyebrows, and I feel the tension drain from them. I hadn't even realized I'd wrinkled it in concentration, trying to figure out where he was, what was next.

"On your back," he says, and I obey, stretching out against soft sheets. Now I have a better idea of where he is, because of how the bed dips under his weight, and he's next to me, kneeling probably.

A cold drip lands on the underside of a breast and I gasp in surprise, and then there's another, and another, and I realize in one of the silences he went and got ice from the kitchen. It's been forever since we played with temperature. He presses a cube against my skin, drawing patterns on my stomach and then around my breasts. I arch up against the bed as the ice leaves goosebumps in its wake, summiting the peak of one breast and then the other. Then it slides down my stomach, below my belly button. It stops, but the melting water doesn't, and it drips between my legs, along my folds. Instinctually I spread my legs further, my body conflicted by my clit's desperate need for attention and complete aversion to the ice. My heart is hammering and my pussy is tingling with anticipation. It wants warm fingers, a warm tongue, friction, heat, but Alec gives me none of those, just freezing cold drips of water that heighten every sensation.

Then his mouth envelops a breast, suckling my skin, teeth lightly scraping my nipple as his scruff scratches the valley between them. His hand slides down between my legs and it's both hot *and* cold, and I don't know how he managed that, but a finger brushes against my clit with a firm touch and somehow that's enough.

Without even trying, I come.

I know I'm not supposed to talk, but still, I moan loudly as I'm hit with it, fingers scrambling against the sheets for purchase as a shudder rocks through me.

I don't know what just happened. I've come but I'm still not satiated, I still need more, and I sit up, pulling the blindfold off me. Alec is lying on his side next to me, naked, unable to hide his surprise, and I act on instinct, pushing him down on his back, and throwing a leg over his hips. I grasp his cock and give it a squeeze to level up from half-hard to fully hard, then position it between my legs, against my opening, and slide down on him.

There's no resistance because I'm dripping with need so I don't even wait for my body to adjust to him before I start moving. I take both his hands in one of mine, pinning them above his head, and we both know that if he wanted to fight me off he could do it easily, but he lets me hold him down as I ride him, tits bouncing by his face. His head lifts a couple of inches and he catches my breast with his mouth, the sudden suction and teeth a jolt that gives the best kind of pain-slash-pleasure.

My pussy grips his cock as his mouth works my breast over, releasing with a wet pop, then bobbing until it catches the other one. I shift to grinding my clit against his pelvic bone, finally getting the friction I need as a second orgasm begins to build. He releases my breast and pulls his knees up, feet flat against the bed to give him leverage as he fucks me from below. His ass raises off the bed with each upward thrust, like he's trying to unseat me, and my thighs hug his hips as I do my best not to get bucked off. Our mouths clash together in a hard, hot kiss, and then I bury my face into the crook of his neck, gasping for air.

"Darce," he groans. "Please tell me you're close because I'm not gonna last much longer."

I nod against his neck, squeezing him even tighter, and then let go with a shout as pleasure washes over me for the second time.

He follows me over the cliff a moment later.

Afterwards we just lay there, pressed together and sweaty as we try to catch our breath. He frees his hands from mine and drapes them across my back, and I feel him slide out of me as he softens. My heart is still galloping, but the rest of me is coming down, and I wonder if I could just fall asleep there, stretched out on top of him.

Amazing sex with Alec is nothing new, but this time was different. It *was* butterflies, anticipation, exhilaration, even though what we tried wasn't anything completely novel. Maybe it was just the fact that he listened to what I was saying. Not that he doesn't usually, but a simple conversation turned into action immediately, he went straight into trying something new, shooting for butterflies.

And damn, he succeeded.

After a few minutes he breaks the silence. "I don't think you've been that quiet, ever."

One chuckle escapes me as I fold my arms across his chest, resting my chin on them. "You told me not to talk!"

"Since when do you follow directions that well?"

I shrug. "When properly motivated. Also, I kind of liked not being able to talk."

He wiggles his eyebrows, then laughs, slapping an ass cheek with a sharp smack then grabbing both of them with greedy hands, massaging and squeezing them. Alec rolls us both over so that I'm on my back, him above me, and gives me a kiss, then a second, then a third. Then he moves to my neck, nibbling and sucking, and I giggle as he hits one of my ticklish spots.

"Stop!" I shriek, and he does, grinning down at me, and then getting up and disappearing into the bathroom. He returns with a damp washcloth and settles between my legs, wiping away the evidence of him before settling back next to me, on his side. Gathering me against his chest, he presses a kiss against the crown of my head.

"So that was good?" he asks.

I nod against his skin. "You heard butterflies and decided, *don't mind if I do.*"

"Anything for you," he says, stroking my hair. After a pause, he adds, "Pinning me down was new."

"Sex Goddess Darcy kind of took over," I admit.

"I like it when she takes over."

I let the silence settle for a moment, trying to figure out whether to say the thoughts swirling around my brain. Sometimes I *hate* sharing my insecurities. *Fake it until you make it* is so much easier.

But I should. Especially with Alec. "You seemed to enjoy it with Rafael, so I kind of wanted to try."

His hand gathers my hair into a ponytail, and tugs lightly so that I have to pull my face away from his chest and look up at him. He says nothing for a minute, eyes tracing my face as if he's trying to read something there. "I like it with you, too."

I nod slowly. "Good."

Even though I'm trying not to let my insecurity show on my face, I must not be doing a very good job, because his forehead wrinkles just the tiniest bit. "Are you okay that I liked it with Rafael?"

"I want you to enjoy what you do with him," I say.

He notices my sidestep. "That's not an answer."

"It kind of is."

He doesn't say anything, so I continue. "I think sometimes I get... jealous isn't the right word, but it's something jealous-adjacent. But overall, yes, I'm not only okay that you have fun with him, I'm happy you do. I want it for you."

"I only want this if you're totally comfortable with it. If this jealous adjacent feeling is too much, if it's going to add any kind of stress or strain to what we have... you know that one word from you and this stops, right? You can safe out even if you're just watching."

"I know," I say. "I would if I needed to, but I don't. If that ever changes, I will, though. I promise."

He nods, and then cups my cheek with one hand, his thumb stroking the soft skin there. I turn my head to press a kiss against his palm, and when I turn back he kisses me. It's soft and sweet, none of the playfulness we usually have with each other. It doesn't lead anywhere, it's just a kiss for the sake of being a kiss, and it reminds me of the ones that we've had at important junctures in our relationship. When we said I love you for the first time. When the giddiness of saying yes to his marriage proposal settled down and we realized what it meant. After giving birth to our oldest.

"Butterflies came back," I say quietly and one chuckle escapes him, jostling his chest.

Then he lets go of me long enough to pull the sheets down and then back up around us. He gathers me in his arms again, and we just lay there, content.

***

I'm not sure how much time has passed when I wake up to Bex sneaking into bed, snuggling at my back.

"Hey," I say sleepily and she presses a kiss to my bare shoulder, wrapping her arms around my waist.

"Didn't mean to wake you," she whispers, and I hear Alec's sleep-rough voice having a similar conversation with Rafael.

"It's fine," I say, turning towards her and stroking her arm with my hand. Then I lower my voice. "Well?"

The room is dark but I can still see her shy smile, her tiny nod. "It was good."

"I get more details than that, right?"

She chuckles quietly, reaching up to tuck a strand of hair behind my ear. "Yeah, but tomorrow. Go back to sleep."

"I'm not–" I start, but the words are cut off by a yawn, completely invalidating the protest I was about to make.

"You are," she argues back, then presses a light kiss to the tip of my nose. "Sleep. I promise to give you all the dirt in the morning."

Chapter 12

THE SUN STREAMING THROUGH the window wakes me up. It's just Bex and I in bed, and the door is cracked. Outside the room I can hear the sounds of the guys talking and moving around the kitchen.

Bex is flung out on her back, hair fanned across the pillow and tits just barely covered by the sheets. I'm tempted to lean over and wake her up with my hands or my mouth, but decide instead to just let her sleep, stretching out next to her and studying how peaceful her face looks, and the way her chest raises and lowers with each breath.

It's just a few minutes later when her breathing shifts and she stretches, eyes fluttering open.

"Morning, beautiful," I tell her, and she turns to look at me, slipping a hand under her pillow.

"Morning yourself," she says sleepily, then sighs, content. "What time is it?"

"Not sure," I admit. "Just woke up, and decided to enjoy the view instead of doing anything productive."

Her cheeks flush pink but she grins, obviously happy. "You just stuck around because you wanted the tea from last night as soon as possible."

"I didn't!" I complain, laughing. "I mean, I *do*, but that's not why I stayed. I stayed because I like you."

"I like you too," she says, and there's a flash of something more serious under her comment, an earnestness tinged with vulnerability. Is this the first time we've said that? It can't be, can it? But then it's gone, and she grins again. "Which is why I'll spill."

"Yesssss," I say, wiggling closer to her and tangling my legs with hers. "I'm all ears."

"Well, it turned out Rafe was half hard all evening thinking about it, which I realized because he pinned me against the door the moment we got into the room. So we jumped each other immediately, just to get it out of the way."

"Just to get it out of the way?" I repeat, raising my eyebrows, and she laughs, waving me off.

"You know what I mean! To settle our nerves, and loosen us up. Also, so that he'd last longer once we really got down to business. And it was good! Sixty-nine, sex, all the good stuff."

"Butterflies?" I ask, and she nods.

"Definitely. And then we got out the lube and got his finger all slick, and started with that."

"And?"

"It was weird. Not bad-weird, just... weird-weird. And felt dirty, but in a good way."

"Bad girl!" I say, and she flushes bright red, covering her face with her hands.

"He called me that," she admits.

"Did you spontaneously orgasm?"

"No... but I did like it. Just as much as I like when he calls me a good girl. Let's face it, though, Rafe could call me just about anything and I'd be putty in his hands."

And she continues, telling me about how he worked her open with his fingers, they slipped the butt plug inside, and then she did the same for him. How the vibration on his toy was too much for him, but once they turned it off and just used it as a butt plug they had sex that was intense and great in a new and different way. It's funny, how this feels like any other of the hundreds of sex gossip sessions we've had over our twenty years of friendship, except this time we're naked in bed together, legs threaded together, while our husbands are outside the door at least somewhat undressed, very possibly kissing or touching or doing who knows what together.

It really is a little mind-blowing how easily this has slipped into our friendship, into our life. Because it doesn't feel weird or awkward to be talking to her about this, even knowing what she and I did together yesterday and what we'll be doing again later today. And I also don't feel any kind of jealousy about her and Rafael.

"He's really curious about anal now," she continues. "Not just with me, though obviously it's probably not a great idea to go from nothing in your ass to coke-can-Alec in your ass in a matter of just a few days."

My stomach flips, because there it is, that thing that I don't have when I think about Rafael and Bex fucking, but I apparently do have when talking about Rafael and Alec fucking.

Jealousy.

I laugh, though I know it sounds strained. "Yeah, probably something to work up to. Bigger butt plugs, more prep beforehand."

"Not something for this trip," she agrees, and I nod, a small wave of relief that I'll have time to get used to the idea.

But Bex tilts her head, studying me. "What aren't you saying?"

Of course she can tell. I guess that's one of the downsides of doing this with someone who can read you like a book. It means they can read you like a book, even when you'd rather they not.

"I don't know," I admit. "Something about them having sex feels weird in a way that hand jobs and blow jobs don't."

She considers that for a moment. "Do you not want them to?"

"I don't think I'd go that far? But I don't know," I repeat, knowing that this time there's a little whine to my voice. "I'm just glad I'll have some time to get used to the idea. Maybe I'll have a better handle on how I feel later."

She nods, and we're both quiet for a bit as we hear the guys in the kitchen. I'm about to suggest we join them when she starts talking again.

"Last year I was the one freaking out a bit," she says, and I nod, remembering. "So before inviting you guys along this time, we talked a lot. Did some reading on ethical non-monogamy. On jealousy, which is normal. I told him about how when he and Alec first made out I had a little freak out, because it went from theoretical to being real. You helped talk me down from that."

"Yeah," I say, sliding my arm around her waist and tangling our legs a little more.

"There's this concept called 'compersion'--have you heard of it?"

When I shake my head, she continues. "People say it's kind of the opposite of jealousy. It's when you're happy that your partner is enjoying themselves with someone else. Genuinely supporting them, even when you don't get anything out of it."

"I get that," I say. "I mean, I think I feel it sometimes. There are things he can get from Rafael that he can't get from me. And sometimes I don't love the way that feels, but there are times when I really want him to get those things, even if it's from someone else."

Bex nods. "Yeah. Neither Rafe nor I explored our bisexuality before we started dating. I mean, Rafe hadn't even realized it, and I was only just starting to when we got together. So what I get from you—both the intimacy and the physicality—is something special. And the same is true for Rafe and Alec."

I nod, thinking over that, and she continues.

"Also, there are tons of things I got from you before last year that I didn't get from Rafe. Because you're a better listener about some things, or the experiences you have make you better to bounce certain stuff off of. Also, I need somewhere to vent about him, because it's just mean to complain *to* him *about* him."

I laugh and nod. "Also chick flicks, and parenting advice, and marriage advice and... all the advice, really. You keep me together when I'm between therapists."

She grins. "And you me. I don't know about you, but I don't think people need partners that complete them—they need villages that do. For some of us partners are a big part of that, but they're not the only part. Rafe and Alec and you and I already did that for each other in other ways. Now we've added a new way. And I think one of the reasons we were able to add this in so seamlessly is because we had that foundation."

Everything she's saying makes sense, and it mollifies me a bit. "Maybe I need to think of it that way, instead of letting my jealousy get too loud."

"I don't think you should ignore the jealousy completely. But try and figure out what's at the root of it, and also pay attention to the parts of their relationship that make you happy."

"Or horny," I say, and she laughs and nods.

"Or horny."

I cup her cheek with my hand, stroking the soft skin there with my thumb. There is so much about her that captures me.

"Thanks," I say seriously, and she looks at me just as seriously.

"You're welcome."

I lean forward to kiss her, tasting her mouth as her hands slide up my back in long strokes. I've just pushed her on her back, hovering over her, when the bedroom door opens.

"We're busy!" I yell, then focus my attention on the spot behind her ear that always elicits a reaction, and I'm rewarded with a whimper.

"But breakfast in bed," Alec says, and I sigh, lifting my head to look at Bex. She reluctantly nods, and I hoist myself off her with an exaggerated aggrieved grunt.

"I *guess*," I say, adjusting the pillows so that I can lean against the headboard, and the guys come over, each settling a legged breakfast tray across our laps.

"French toast!" Bex exclaims, and Rafael leans over to give her a kiss.

"I was supposed to be doing that," I grumble good-naturedly, and then study the tray and look at Alec. "I guess this'll do."

"Brat," he teases, sitting next to me and stealing a piece of bacon, taking a bite out of it as I swipe at his hands.

"Yeah. I probably deserve a spanking," I say, and he grins.

"Later," he promises, and leans in and gives me my own kiss.

Chapter 13

AFTER BREAKFAST WE GET ready for the day, plans for which include a tour of the local wineries. Alec has offered to drive, leaving the other three of us to imbibe as much as we want, though teetering on the edge of forty means that we need to have *some* limits. We don't want to waste one of our precious vacation days with a hangover.

Still, we have fun and let loose in a way that we haven't for a while. A couple of glasses in and I've turned my flirt on, with both Alec and Bex on the receiving end.

"Not feeling left out, are you?" I ask Rafael as Alec ducks into a cheese shop to retrieve a charcuterie board we ordered before the next stop. I wink at him, and the smirk he gives me in return makes my stomach flutter momentarily.

"Hey Bex," I stage whisper. "Your husband has a hot smirk."

"Hey Darce," she whispers back. "Your husband has a hot everything."

We dissolve into giggles as Alec gets back into the car and looks at us, amused.

"What are you guys talking about?" he asks.

"Your abs, probably," Rafael says with his dead-sexy smirk, and Bex and I glance at each other and give a knowing nod. Because my husband's abs are amazing.

"And the way they cut down," I say, making a gesture that suggests his Adonis belt, and then reach over the center console to untuck his shirt.

But he catches my hands, laughing, and settles me back into my seat, leaning over to put my seatbelt on. "Hands to yourself, young lady!" he says, and I grumble, but stay put.

At the next stop we munch on the meats and cheeses and crackers that Alec bought while we sip on another glass, and then are encouraged to down some water. I'm in that place of the perfect buzz, where the world is happy and soft around the edges, and I'm with my favorite people in the world. I can't imagine an afternoon more perfect.

Especially when Bex and I sneak away to make out against the side of a building. We're out of sight of the crowds and the kisses are lazy, indulgent, with some slight wandering of hands. Alec finds us eventually, leaning his shoulder against the side of the building and crossing his arms across his chest. When we pull apart he's watching us, one eyebrow raised.

"Making out like a couple of teenagers," he says, and Bex giggles, nodding.

"Guilty."

"Jealous?" I ask, tossing my hair over my shoulder.

In a flash I'm the one against the wall, the sun-warmed stucco pressing against my breasts. He's at my back, his chest sturdy against my shoulder blades. And against my ass his cock is making its presence known, probing, insistent.

"A little, yeah," he says quietly. "I could take you right here, you know. Hike your skirt up, shove your panties to the side, slide up into you."

"I'd like that," I say, sounding more breathless than I expected. My panties were already damp, but now they're moreso.

"I'll stand guard," Bex offers, and when I glance at her I see eyes full of lust, a heaving chest.

But then there's air against my back. Alec has taken a step back. "Maybe later," he says casually, and I groan, letting my head drop back against the wall.

"Tease!"

When I glance back at him he nods, one hand reaching down to adjust himself through his jeans, and he's so hot that I almost can't stand it. Then he walks back towards the crowd as I groan again.

"Damn," Bex says leaning against the wall next to me, and I drop my head against her shoulder. "Your husband is..."

I just nod.

"You're going to get fucked so good when we get back," she says, and I nod again, taking her hand and tugging her back to the tables.

***

The rest of the afternoon goes by in a blur, and I spend most of it making sex eyes at Alec, who swaps between making them back, and pretending to ignore me completely and focusing his attention on Rafael and Bex. They eat it up, and Bex in particular thinks it's hilarious, playing up the flirty glances, and leaning forward so that her cleavage is fully on display for him—but also me. Which leaves me torn between making sex eyes at Alec and making sex eyes at Bex's tits.

So it shouldn't really be a surprise that once we've pulled away from the last place and are on an empty country road back to the house, I pounce. I reach over the center console and pop the button of his fly open, then wiggle down the zipper.

"Darcy," he says warningly, but still slides his legs apart, making it easier for me to reach in and grasp his cock.

"Hmmmm?" I ask, dragging fingers over the skin that's quickly growing taut.

"I'm driving," he says, but interrupts himself with a groan when I grasp him and give a little squeeze.

"Then keep your eyes on the road," I reply with a shrug. I swirl my thumb across the tip of his cock, where precum is gathering, then reach back for Rafael.

"Wanna taste?" I ask, and he gives another panty-dropping smirk, leaning forward to capture my thumb between his lips. I feel the rough surface of his tongue against the pad of my thumb as he sucks my finger clean.

It shouldn't be so hot, but it is. When I glance at Bex her eyes are locked on Rafael's mouth, and she's licking her lips. "Use your mouth to lube her up for him," she suggests, then glances at me. I nod at her, and then at him, heart pounding. He gently grasps my wrist and laps at my palm, my fingers, until it's shiny with his spit, and when he lets go I reach over for Alec, grasping his cock once again.

Another groan escapes from him. He leans over and whispers in my ear how that was so fucking hot, that *I'm* so fucking hot. I'm a little breathless, the echo of Rafael's tongue making my palm tingle, and nod in agreement, giving his cock a squeeze as I think about the grip Rafael had on my wrist.

A deep breath to focus on my husband, and I start stroking his cock. Alec's teeth bite down on his bottom lip so hard it starts to turn white. Another groan fills the car, but this time it's from the back seat, and when I look back there Bex is leaned over, mouth filled with Rafael's cock. He's pulled her hair back, clutching it into a messy ponytail, and his hips are just barely hitching up each time her mouth slides down.

"Don't think my mouth can reach you," I say apologetically to Alec, gesturing at the center console with my free hand, and he just shakes his head.

"Love your hand," he grunts.

Alec manages to keep driving as I continue the hand job, as Rafael's breathing speeds up, as he whispers to Bex that he's close. I look back at them in time to see her nod as she continues to suck him off. His hips speed up as does her head, and then he freezes, the fist around her hair jerking lightly. She makes a quiet noise and he releases her immediately.

"Sorry, sorry," he says, as she sits up and grins, shaking her head and wiping at her mouth with the back of her hand.

"Nothing to be sorry for."

As he chuckles and gives her a kiss I turn back on Alec, whose own breathing is becoming a bit more ragged.

"You good to do this while driving?" I ask, and he nods, reaching for the stash of fast-food napkins we have stowed away.

I position them to catch his release with my free hand, then speed up my other hand's movements as his own thrusting becomes less controlled.

"Fuck, Darce," he grits between clenched teeth, and I lean forward so that my mouth is against his ear.

"Do it."

He does.

Chapter 14

WHEN WE GET TO the house, I make a beeline for Bex and Rafael's bathroom, stripping off clothes as I go.

"It sounds like y'all didn't use the bathtub last night, and we are *not* letting it go to waste," I say, leaning over the edge to plug up the drain. My bare ass in the air, someone bumps against me, and when I look back I see Alec, pants around his ankles and cock in hand as he playfully prods me with it. "Gotta get me ready first," I say, and he just grins and holds up a bottle of silicone lube.

"I came prepared."

Then he reaches down and sweeps me off my feet, arm under the back of my knees. I wrap my arms around his neck, laughing as I kiss him.

"Turn on the water," he mutters against my mouth, and after I do, Bex reaches over to test the temperature, adjusting until it's just right. Alec sets me down inside the tub, and I reach over to help a naked Bex in. The guys finish pulling off their own clothes and join us a moment later.

"This is basically a hot tub," Rafael says, and Alec nods, sitting down and pulling me sideways onto his lap, arms draped around my waist.

"It was *made* for group sex. This whole place was."

"We should come here every year," Bex says, resting her cheek on Rafael's shoulder, and he grins, pressing a kiss to the top of head.

"If this is what we found for our first time, imagine all the other places out there, though?"

I glance up at Alec, and can see that he has the same question I do.

Every year?

His eyes also scream the answer that my mind immediately jumped to.

Fuck yes.

I clear my throat. "So we're doing this every year, then?"

Bex flushes pink as her gaze meets mine. "Oh, I guess we didn't actually discuss that. But... I really like this."

"I do too," I agree.

"Would we just go back to normal in between?" Alec asks.

"I think we need to," Rafael says. "The kids... the *everyone*, really."

"Can you imagine the gossip if this got out?" Bex asks, and my immediate instinct is to say to fuck the gossip, it's none of their business. But they're right.

"But if we keep it quiet," I ask. "We can keep doing it?"

Bex and Rafael look at each other, then back at us, and nod. Grinning, I make my way to Bex, kneeling between her knees and cupping her chin.

"Good," I say before pulling her in for a kiss.

I straddle her lap and we make out for a bit while Rafael crosses the tub to Alec and they do the same. The guys take it up to the next level first, and I glance over when I hear the top of the lube flip open. They're kneeling on a seat, Alec with both of their cocks in his grip, and Rafael drizzling the silicone liquid on and around Alec's moving fist.

I turn around and sit between Bex's spread legs as Rafael groans "Fuuuuck," thrusting up into Alec's grasp. Their cocks rub against each other in a different tempo from his stroke, but after a minute they get in sync, fucking Alec's hand together as they kiss. Then their breaths start coming faster as everything speeds up, groans and swears slipping out, and suddenly come at almost the exact same time. Bex's thighs squeeze my hips as Alec bites down on Rafael's shoulder, choking down a groan, and Rafael lets out a string of swears.

When they finally separate there's a circle of teeth marks on Rafael's skin.

"Vampire," I tease, wiping down Alec's torso with a washcloth, and he leans down and plants his teeth on my shoulder, leaving me with a circle of indentations of my own.

"Well now I feel left out," Bex says when he pulls away, and he laughs, taking her hand and tugging her toward him as the water swishes around them. Back to his chest, he drapes an arm around her waist and I reach over to swipe all her hair over one shoulder so that he can bend his head down to mark her as well. As I watch, she shivers against him, and I momentarily wonder if this is crossing a line, if I should feel jealous. But I don't, and when I glance over at Rafael he doesn't seem to be either. If anything, he looks turned on, a lustful gleam in his eyes.

"You *bit* me!" she squeals when he releases her, but it's playful, as is the growl he replies with that sends her splashing back into Rafael's arms, who is laughing.

"We've all been marked," I say. "Guess that means you're Alpha."

"We'll see about that," Rafael argues, a challenge in his eyes, but he's mollified when Bex straddles his lap and kisses him.

Alec pulls me towards him as well, but after a bit more kissing he breaks away, reaching for the soap that's sitting on the edge of the tub.

"Speaking of anal," he says, passing the soap to me, and I laugh as I take it.

"Were we talking about anal?"

"We are now. Pass that to Bex when you're done."

Bex looks a little nervous as I pass it to her.

"Relax," I tell her, brushing my lips against hers. "I don't know what he's thinking, but whatever it is, you guys can always pass."

She nods, looking just a hair less nervous as Alec tugs me away, then situates me so that I'm kneeling on one of the seats, turned away from him. Gently pressing between my shoulder blades, I bend over, resting my arms on the ledge so that my ass is in the air, and one of his hands rests on my lower back, thumb rubbing circles on the skin there.

"Up," he says from somewhere behind me, and the water ripples as Bex settles next to me in the same position. Her lower lip is caught between her teeth, and I'm not the only one who can tell she's nervous, because Alec's other hand comes to rest on her lower back, fingers tracing the same pattern as they are on me. "It's just us."

"They're good nerves," she clarifies as Alec drops his hand and Rafael settles behind her.

"Good," Alec says. "And like Darcy said, you can always pass. But Rafael said you guys were curious about rim jobs."

Bex turns pink but nods, and Alec kneels behind me, taking a light nibble out of one cheek before placing his hands on my ass, spreading me open for him. "Try to relax, and I'll show him how it's done."

She nods, chest expanding and contracting with a deep breath, and crosses her arms on the tile, resting her head on them. I do the same as Alec begins giving instructions behind me.

"It's like oral, in that I tease a lot first. Don't go straight to home plate." His tongue dances across my backside, teeth occasionally nipping at a cheek, fingers running along my inner thighs with the errant brush against my clit.

Next to me I can actually see Bex relaxing–the tension draining from her shoulders, the crease between her eyebrows disappearing. Her breathing evens out and a small smile is playing across her face when her eyes suddenly fly open. "Oh."

"Good oh?" asks Rafael. "Do you like it?"

Bex pauses for a moment, and the crease between her eyebrows appears again. "I think so?"

"That's not convincing, mi vida. Do you want me to stop?"

"I-I don't think so," she says, turning pink again. "It's just... it feels like something I'm not *supposed* to like."

"But you do?" he asks, and another sharp intake of breath comes from her as she nods.

"I do," she admits, and he must end his teasing because her breath speeds up from its previously relaxed and calm pace.

Alec, too, switches from teasing to the main event, tongue flat against me, and then a little probing. I reach down to grab one of my tits, cupping and stroking and tugging as he hits all the spots he knows rev my engine. Then Bex reaches for me, batting my hand away and replacing it with hers.

I've never been able to come from this, but it's still heady as fuck, arousal coursing through my body. Bex seems to be having the same reaction, and I reach for the tit of hers that's in my reach, and when I pinch a nipple her eyes fly open with a groan.

"Gonna come?" I ask, and she shakes her head.

"I don't think so. God this feels so good, but it's not *orgasm* good, you know?"

I nod because I do know. Alec's mouth leaves my ass and as he pulls up to full height I hear the top of the lube flip open again. Rafael does the same, and then I feel Alec's cock notched against my pussy, a lubed up thumb probing my asshole. Somehow he's ready again.

"Can I?" he asks, and I nod, almost desperately.

"Please."

Slowly his thumb penetrates and seats itself in my ass as his cock settles deep in my pussy.

"Mi vida?" Rafael asks, and Bex's answer is more tentative.

"I think so?"

His shape comes into view as he leans over her.

"I can skip the thumb, amor. We can wait until you're sure."

"No, I..." Her chest heaves in another deep breath. "I'm sure, it just... feels weird to say so. Because you're not supposed to."

"Says who?" I argue. "I love all sorts of things people say you're not *supposed* to. I love anal. I love getting on my knees for Alec and giving him a blow job. I love being a little tipsy and high and him tossing me around a bit. I also love going down on you. I love the way you shudder and groan, and I really love watching you and Rafael together. And I... ugh." I glare back at Alec, who wiggled his thumb a bit in my ass and completely distracted me. "I'm trying to give a pep talk here!"

He shrugs, looking not at all sorry, and Bex laughs, sounding and looking lighter.

She glances back at Rafael. "Do it? While you fuck me?"

"God it's hot when you ask for it," he replies, and I can tell the moment his thumb breaches past the outer rim of muscle from the inelegant "Umphf" that escapes from her. Another moan comes when he's slid his cock in fully.

"Damn," she groans as he begins to move, and Alec thrusts into me as well. Reaching out, Bex wraps her hand around the back of my neck, pulling me in for a kiss.

Kissing Bex while Alec fucks me is beyond amazing. Her tongue tangles with mine as he rams into me from behind. Her hand wraps around my hair as his grips my hip. His thumb probes me as her teeth nibble at my lips.

It's decadent, sinfully good.

One of my hands reaches for her tit, thumb brushing against a nipple which pebbles in response. A light pinch rewards me with a quiet groan into my mouth, when I go harder, she gets louder. I pull away and duck down to draw her into my mouth, worshiping her breast with my lips, tongue, and teeth in turn.

"Shit," she whimpers, the hand in my hair tightening, and the tingle of pain that comes with that just heightens every other sensation coursing through my body.

A muffled moan from behind me draws my attention, and when I glance back, I see the guys are kissing too. I watch them for a moment, fascinated by the way Rafael's forearm and bicep are tensed as they grip Bex's hip. The way the V of Alec's Adonis belt disappears behind me, but I know it's pointing at the cock that's fucking me thoroughly.

Alec groans again and I know that groan, it means he's close. Resting my forehead on one forearm, I reach my other hand between my legs and start stroking myself so that we can come together. Bex sweeps my hair off my shoulder and kisses me there, then on my neck, then nibbles on my earlobe.

"God you're gorgeous," she whispers in my ear. "Body all tensed, right on the edge. Can't wait to see you come, hear you as your orgasm washes over you and you can't hold yourself back."

Every time Alec shoves into me another whimper escapes, louder and louder as I approach my peak. Alec slaps my ass and the sting almost does me in.

"You like that, baby?" he asks. "You ready for me to fill you up?"

"Please," I beg. "I'm almost there."

Then Rafael's voice cuts in, a growl that is pure sex in itself. "Come in your wife," he orders.

It's him that sends me over the edge, and my pussy squeezing is what finishes Alec off. Buried deep in me, his body stutters, short aftershocks as I continue to pulse around him.

Gasping, we collapse back into the bathtub as Rafael continues to fuck Bex. Alec is behind him, hands gripping his waist, probably licking his ass based on the way Rafael's eyes have rolled back in his head.

Bex usually isn't as loud as I am when she comes, but I know her breath patterns, the way her body moves when she's close. Sliding next to her I tuck a strand of hair behind her ear and reach between her legs to stroke her.

"Now it's your turn, baby. I want to see you come."

She turns her head to look at me, and there's something soft and vulnerable in her eyes. It's like I can sense the emotions she's feeling, the depth and breadth of them, and I wonder for a moment whether that's a look for Rafael, or if it's one for me. And I realize I want at least some of it for me. She leans forward and brushes her lips against mine, then nods and closes her eyes.

"I'm gonna," she whispers, voice hoarse.

One hand fondling her clit, I cup her cheek with my other hand, stroking her soft skin with my thumb. "Good girl."

She gasps and comes, followed a moment later by Rafael whose pace slows but still continues through his orgasm until he can't anymore and then pulls out of her, dropping to his knees. The water sloshes around the bath, and we're all still and quiet for a few minutes as we recover.

"That was..." Bex says, finally breaking the silence.

"Okay, I *guess*," I finish with a smirk, and she leans over to shove me in the shoulder, though she's grinning.

"But seriously, how does it just keep getting *better*?" she asks, and Alec shrugs.

"Think there's a ceiling?"

"Not sure but I'm open to trying to find it."

"You guys came *three times* today," I say, shaking my head. "What do they put in the water here, and can we bottle it?"

"What can I say," Rafael replies. "I feel eighteen again."

Chapter 15

THE NEXT DAY IS our last full day, and while part of me wants to make the most of it and spend it in bed, Rafael convinces us to mini-golf.

Yes, mini-golf.

"This is so cheesy," Bex says, laughing as we get in the car, and Rafe wraps his arm around her waist, pulling her into his lap.

"The kids are going to ask what we did on our vacation, and we don't have nearly enough family-friendly pictures."

"It's not like we have family un-friendly ones instead," she says, and I grin.

"Yet."

When we piled into bed last night, Alec brought up taking x-rated pictures of Bex and Rafael again, and Bex blushed bright red, but nodded.

"We talked, and think it'd be fun?" she said, her voice lilting at the end as if she was unsure. "I've always thought couples boudoir was hot, but also super intimidating. It would be less intimidating with you guys there."

"Since we've already seen you naked," Alec said.

"Since we've already seen you *fucking*," I added, and Bex grinned and nodded.

"So yeah, let's," she said, as Rafael's arm snaked around her, hand cupping her breast and giving a little squeeze.

Back in the car on the way to minigolf, Rafael smirked. "Last year you took pictures of us dry humping against a railing on a nature walk, might as well one-up it this year."

I can't believe the vacation is almost over, and I have no idea how to go home tomorrow and pretend like none of this happened. Last time it was easier because we just fell into it, but we don't have that excuse this time. We've even talked about doing this regularly–but the expectation to go back to life as usual in between? I know that's what Rafael wants, and I don't know what the alternative is, but I do know that pretending like the only feelings I have for Bex are nonsexual platonic ones is going to be much harder this time.

Luckily we arrive before I can descend too far into the what-ifs. And while I'm not particularly good at minigolf, it turns out Bex is even worse than I am. The first hole is meant to be easy, a starter hole, but when her third stroke goes wide, she bursts into giggles.

"I'm hopeless!" she says as Rafael steps behind her, wrapping his arms around her and placing his hands over hers.

"Don't hit it too hard," he says. "Back, and then just a tap."

This time she sinks it, and I mark her '4' next to my '3' and the '1' that both guys earned.

"Here, let me try," I say when I sink the next hole in two but Bex is still going.

"You're not much better than I am!" she counters, though when I slide my arms around her she grins at me over her shoulder. "Oh, your helping me has nothing to do with golf, does it?"

"How dare you!" I say, closing my hand over hers. "It has everything to do with teaching you how to stroke."

"She's pretty good at stroking," Rafael says, and I toss my hair over my shoulder, as Bex's ball goes wide.

"Bet I'm better," I say.

"Bet you're not," she counters.

"Looks like I finished in two, and you're going to end up with twice that."

"That's your fault!"

"Too many hands," I say with a shrug, and Alec cuts in, shaking his head.

"No such thing. The more hands the better."

"Yeah?" I ask. Then I get mental image of Alec fucking me with his fingers while Bex sits behind me, playing with my tits, and I shudder, answering my own question. "Okay, yeah."

"Penny for your thoughts," says Rafael with a smirk as his golf ball rolls into the frog's mouth and sinks into the hole.

"It's not for public consumption," I say, as I miss another shot and Alec snorts with laughter.

"Watch yourself," I say over my shoulder, giving him a glare, but he winks at me instead, completely unintimidated.

"Or what?"

"Or I'll get you back later."

He wiggles his eyebrows, smirking. "Can't wait."

The next hole has a roller coaster style loop-de-loop, and Bex just stares. But Rafael comes up behind her, brushing his lips against the spot where her neck and shoulder meet.

"If you get it, I'll reward you later."

"Well that's proper motivation," she says, placing her ball and taking a deep breath. It makes it through the loop, but doesn't sink into the hole until her second stroke.

"Close enough," Rafael says, and Bex pumps her fist in victory.

I am not nearly as successful though, first hitting it too soft, and then too hard. The third attempt makes it through, but then it takes another two to sink the ball into the hole, and I mark a 5 next to my name.

"You know the goal is lowest points, right?" Alec says, and I poke him in the thigh with my club.

"Maybe my goal is different! Maybe I want the highest points!"

The game continues much the same, the guys hitting par almost every time, while Bex and I mostly double it. Teasing and snark and stolen touches. Stolen kisses too, but those are just between Alec and me, or Bex and Rafael.

As Rafael and Bex banter back and forth, stepping closer and closer until they kiss, I watch them, wondering what it would be like to kiss her out in the open, where anyone could see. Obviously I won't. Obviously what we have is for behind closed doors, where everyone understands and is on the same page. Kissing someone other than Alec right now isn't in the cards, even if we're an hour from home, away from anyone that could recognize us.

But I'll kiss the fuck out of her in private, and work on being okay that's the only place I get her.

Hands settle on my hips and it's Alec who comes up behind me. Mouth next to my ear he whispers, "Knock knock."

I laugh and roll my eyes, turning to him. "Who's there?"

"Can I come in?"

"Can I come in who?"

He breaks into a grin, then mouths *you*.

Groaning, I shake my head as he wraps his arms around me. "That's bad."

"So yes?" he asks, pressing my pelvis against him where I can feel him half-hard.

"Sir, we are in public!" I say, but I can't help laughing as I push him away. "Save that for the bedroom."

"Fine," he grumbles as we approach the windmill.

"I'm not even going to try," I say, throwing my hands up when it takes Rafael three attempts to get past the windmill's blades.

"C'mon," Bex says, bumping her shoulder against mine. "Give it a shot."

"Fine," I grumble, placing my ball down, and when I stand up, Bex is standing behind me. She wraps her arms around me, covering my hands with hers.

"Back... and... there!" she says, tapping the ball. Miraculously it slips in between the windmill blades and...

"Seriously?!" Alec exclaims. "You seriously just got a hole in one?"

"Dream team!" I say, raising my hand up for a high five. Bex hesitates for a moment, eyes trained on my mouth, but then raises her hand up to slap mine.

"Like you said earlier," she adds. "Four hands are better than two."

"Good job, mi vida," Rafael says, planting a kiss on her temple, and this time when her eyes linger on his mouth, she closes the gap between them and kisses him. Because they can.

The scores at the end of the game are unsurprising–Alec and Rafael have low scores, Bex and I have sky-high ones. In the end Rafael edged Alec out by just one point, and when he tosses us a smirk I notice that Alec's eyes are drawn to his mouth, too.

We pile back into the car, stopping at a brewery for lunch where I finagle the seating arrangement so that I can sit between Bex and Alec, with Rafael across from me. We're in a corner of the room, so when I slip my hand under the table and squeeze Bex's knee, she flushes but doesn't move, instead covering my hand with hers.

What's it going to be like when we go home this time? Last time we'd made it clear that this was a one-time thing, so after a bit of awkwardness, we returned to life as it was before we'd hooked up. But this time, after the conversation we had where we admitted that we want to do it again, how do we navigate life back home? Is the rule hands off when we're in Austin, but anything goes on vacation? And if that's the case, can we go on vacation once a month?

"Earth to Darcy!" Alec says, shaking me out of my thoughts.

"Sorry, was distracted," I apologize, and he studies me for a moment.

"Want to share?" Rafael asks, but just then the waitress reappears with our food. Which I'm grateful for, because I need to sort out my thoughts before I bring them to everyone.

"Later," I say, and while they exchange glances, nobody pushes the subject, instead digging into their food.

Chapter 16

The conversation during the car ride back is about the photos Alec is going to take, so when we get there Rafael and Bex disappear into their room while Alec gets out his camera and lenses and brings them to the room where we've been sleeping. I make up the bed again, laying out a loosely knit throw blanket and doing my best to set up a background that looks neatly situated, but won't draw attention away from the focus of the pictures.

But when Bex shows up in the doorway wearing a teal lace bra and panties set, Rafael next to her in snug black boxer briefs I know anyone who looks at those pictures will be so distracted by them there could be a celebrity in the background and no one would notice.

"Damn," I say, staring openly at each of them in turn. "Y'all are fucking on fire."

Bex blushes but accepts the compliment, walking into the room and tugging Rafael with her. "Okay, so what do we do?"

"Whatever you want," Alec says, and Bex and Rafael look at each other, and then turn away, bursting into laughter.

"This is too much pressure!" Bex says. "I need direction!"

"Kiss him," I suggest, and she goes up on her tiptoes and the kiss they share is sweet, but brief.

"Come *on!*" I exclaim, throwing my hands up in the air, but Alec elbows me in the ribs.

"You're making it worse!" he chides.

"Fine," I say, then study them for a moment, thinking.

"Rafael, reach out and brush a thumb across a boob. Wake one of those nipples up."

He does, and sure enough a bump appears through the lace of her bra as her nipple gets hard. Her eyes flutter shut, and he leans down to kiss the tops of her breasts, where smooth skin meets teal lace.

"Bex, brush the backs of your fingers across that big ole bulge he's got in his boxers. See if you can make him twitch."

She opens her eyes and does, and this time it's his eyes that close. When she does a second time, a quiet groan escapes, and his cock twitches enough that we see it through the fabric.

"Nice," I say approvingly. "Okay, now try that kiss again."

When he opens his eyes and looks at her, I can feel the heat radiating off their connection. His hands rest on her hips, then slide around her waist as he draws her to him. Her arms go up and around his neck, and this time when they kiss it's neither sweet nor short. Their mouths open and there's a flash of tongue, while one of his hands drops down to grab her ass, hauling her against him as he squeezes and kneads the flesh there.

They break apart and then come together for a second kiss, a third, and then Rafael's free hand reaches up to her ponytail, tugging on it so that her neck stretches out and she's forced to look at the ceiling. His mouth attaches itself to the new expanse of skin that's now laid out for him, and he kisses and sucks and nibbles his way from her ear to her collarbone, and then back up. His tongue drags against her skin and I squirm a little, turned on and unable to look away.

"Rafe," she says quietly as he switches to the other side, and I glance over at Alec who's taking pictures, measured pauses between them as he waits for another perfect moment. He meets my gaze when I nod at the tent in his shorts, and he lets out a silent laugh before turning back to the camera.

"Okay," I say, once they slow down. "Now go to the wall. First Bex up against it, then swap and Rafael there."

They follow my directions, Bex leaning against the wall and looking up at him, while Rafael plants his palms on either side of her head, looming over her. They watch each other for a moment, then Bex's hands creep up to his pecs as she stretches up and towards him, and he brings his mouth down to hers.

As time goes on they become more comfortable, and all I have to do is throw out an idea and they run with it. When I tell Bex to get on her knees for him, she does, and what follows are a sequence of photos of her taking off his boxers, of him grasping the back of her head. She worships his cock with her mouth and it makes my own mouth water with desire for a cock, for hands in my hair holding me close as my throat gets fucked.

I remind Rafael that turnabout is fair play, and they move to the bed. She stretches out, arching up as his head dives between her legs. There's a gorgeous shot of her, back bowed, hands buried in his hair, and I'm going to want a copy of that for my own collection.

After he makes her come he crawls up her body, planting kisses along the way, and then she wraps her legs around his waist, drawing him up against her.

"Good to keep taking pictures?" Alec asks quietly, and they glance at him, then me, then back at each other as if they'd forgotten we were in the room. But then Bex nods and Rafael breaks into a grin, reaching down to notch his cock up against her opening.

It looks like they don't really need me anymore, so I just watch as he slides into her, as she sighs and her belly presses up against him. He pulls out and then pushes back in again, and she grasps his ass, encouraging his movements as he continues pumping in and out. His head ducks down to her breasts that were bared somewhere along the way, and the groan that escapes her suggests he uses his teeth more than his lips or tongue.

Watching them is so fucking hot, a live sex show right in front of me, and I sit on the floor near the back wall and slip my hands under my panties. I play with myself as they continue, switching positions so that she's on top, then on her hands and knees as he drives into her from behind. I don't want to distract them, so I try my best to be quiet, teeth clamping my lips shut to avoid making a sound. My breath is coming faster, and as he reaches down and between her legs to stroke her clit, I do the same, moving at the same pace as them. She's on all fours and I am too, except that one of my hands is bringing me closer to the edge as I thrust against it, trying to be silent, trying to keep my breath from being too noisy.

Alec has moved and is now aiming his camera where their bodies meet, where Rafael disappears inside Bex, a soft smacking sound filling the room with every thrust. "Fuck," she whimpers, and he moves his mouth by her ear, whispering things I can't make out. Whatever they are, it's working, though, because I can see the muscles in her thighs tense. She's pushing herself back against him, fucking him as much as he's fucking her, tits swinging as she just repeats the word *fuck* over and over again, as if she's ordering him to keep going.

Then another groan and an "I'm gonna," followed by his "Do it!" And she does, all quiet whimpers as his fingers dig into her hips and thrust a few more times before freezing, cock buried deep in her pussy.

Which is when I let myself come, fingers stroking my g-spot and thumb brushing my clit until all the muscles in my body release and my hand is coated in slick, wet warmth.

The arm that was holding me up gives in, but I don't even care that I've tumbled against the floor face first. I'm just satiated, chest heaving, as I breathe hard. Once I'm recovered I flop to my back, staring at the ceiling until I realize how quiet the room is. And when I glance at the bed Bex and Rafael are looking at me, faces crinkling in an amused smile.

Alec reaches over and grabs my hand, capturing the two fingers that were inside me a moment ago with his mouth. I chuckle weakly as he licks them clean, then glance back up at the bed.

"I didn't distract you, did I? I tried to be quiet."

"Who knew you could be quiet?" Bex says with a grin, stretching out on her stomach as Rafael settles next to her, taking the blanket I'd artfully thrown on the bed and draping it on top of her.

"I mentioned my Herculean efforts earlier! I do my best not to scar the kids, and I did my best not to pull your attention away from your pornographic photo shoot. Priorities."

"Well thank you for thinking of us," Rafael says, and I smirk.

"I think of your wife when I come more often than I should admit." It's a flirty quip, but also accurate.

Bex grins and Alec gives a playful pout before I crawl over to him and settle into his lap.

"I think about you too, babe, don't worry."

Alec holds up the camera and nods to Bex and Rafael. "Want to see how I did?"

They nod, joining us on the floor, and Alec hands them the camera. We peek over their shoulders as they flip through the pictures, Bex giggling nervously and covering her eyes occasionally.

"Holy shit, you're good at this," Rafael says, pausing on a picture of them kissing while he fingers her.

"It helps when the models are stupid hot," Alec says waving a hand with an air of dismissiveness. But I can tell from the way that he's looking at them and their reactions rather than the pictures that he's a little nervous, self-conscious. Every compliment they give results in a flash of a smile, followed by a concerned wrinkle of his brow when they switch to the next picture.

I rest my hand on his thigh, giving it a squeeze, and when he looks at me I mouth *they love them.* He nods and smiles, giving me a little wink and leaning down to press a kiss to my shoulder before turning his attention back to them.

"What do you guys do with the pictures you have?" Bex asks, and Alec shrugs.

"We have a secure messaging app with photo albums where we store them."

"*Not* anywhere they can get mixed up with family pictures," I butt in, then he continues.

"Sometimes I use them when she's not around but I'm not in the mood for standard porn. Sometimes we send them to each other as a 'wanna do this tonight?' flirty message."

"I've thought about printing some of my favorites and making a book or something, but haven't gotten around to it. Maybe one day, when I'm old and wrinkly, to remind myself of how hot I used to be," I add.

"Where would you even get them printed? You'd need somewhere that's discrete, I'm not going to Walgreens."

"Definitely not somewhere local," I agree. "Part of the reason I haven't done it is because I need to do the research."

Bex nods, looking thoughtfully at the camera screen which is paused on a picture of her riding Rafael, her hands cupping and squeezing her breasts while she looks like an absolute goddess.

"You want to print out pictures!" I say, and she blushes but nods, gesturing to the camera.

"I look fucking hot!" she says with a little shrug, and I laugh and nod, reaching over to give her shoulders a squeeze.

"You really fucking do."

Chapter 17

I REALLY CAN'T BELIEVE it's our last day, that come tomorrow we'll be back home back in our normal life, doing normal things. Not that what we're doing isn't normal, it just isn't normal for *us*.

Or it *wasn't* normal for us, until last year.

But maybe it's becoming normal? For us? I don't know if I want that, I don't know if *they* want that, and I don't know, even if we all want that, if it's something we can have.

But at least we have this evening.

We all must be thinking the same thing, because as I'm cleaning up in the kitchen after dinner with Rafael he says, "Sixteen more hours."

I check my watch, and sure enough, he's right. "I'm trying to not be offended that you apparently have a countdown going."

He shakes his head. "Not like that! Just trying to remind myself that it's ending soon. I don't want to get caught off guard tomorrow morning because I lost track of time."

"Yeah."

We're both quiet for a moment, me drying the plates as he hands them to me, before I break the silence. "Wish we could do this more often."

"Not really practical," he says. "Kids and all. Plus, if we start disappearing together too often, people will get suspicious."

"Maybe," I say. "But of what? Do you really think that people are going to assume we're all fucking each other? Maybe they'll think we're spies or something. You think I could pass as a spy?"

"You gossip too much, no one will think you can keep secrets."

I laugh, but he's right. "Little do they know, I'm holding on to one of the juiciest secrets ever. And I've never even considered telling a soul what you and your wife look like when you come."

Rolling his eyes, he elbows me. "And you won't."

"And I won't," I agree, as Bex and Alec bring in the last of the things from the table outside.

"Plans for this evening?" Bex asks.

"Sex," I say, as if that was the dumbest question I've ever heard, and she reaches out and shoves me lightly on the shoulder.

"Just making sure everyone's up for it! We've had a lot of it this week."

"Sore?" I ask. "Need a break?"

She shakes her head, and I break into a grin, because thank goodness.

Rafael takes her hand and tugs her down the hall to Alec's and my bedroom, then the bathroom, reaching in to turn on the shower. Alec and I are right behind them, and when I move to pull off my shirt Alec catches my hands, lightly pinning them behind my back and nudging me towards the streaming water.

Less than a minute and we're both soaked, clothes clinging to every surface and curve of our bodies. Bex and Rafael have joined us, and when Alec releases me to turn to Rafael, I turn to Bex, slipping my hand under the hem of her shirt and touching her warm, wet skin. She grins and when she kisses me I open my mouth up to her, inviting her in. Her tongue sweeps against mine and we only pull apart to tug shirts over our heads, first me undressing her, then her undressing me. Our bottoms are next, her wide leg yoga pants and my leggings. And then she's standing there in front of me, in teal lingerie, hair plastered against her shoulders and back as rivulets of water course down her body.

"You're gorgeous," I say to her, and she flushes, but doesn't break eye contact.

Her voice is quiet. "I'm starting to believe you mean it when you say that."

Something about the way that she's looking at me makes my heart pound, and I nod. "You should."

She kisses me again, this time soft, slow. Like it means something. Our hands wander, over skin, over fabric, then tugging fabric off skin. Our mouths move, nibbling shoulders, licking breasts, tonguing nipples. It feels so natural, being with her, taking turns to elicit sighs and gasps and moans.

The guys are kissing too, and I occasionally see them in the periphery of my vision, but all my attention is focused on Bex, on what we're doing together. She drops to her knees, and I tangle my fingers in her hair as she pulls off my underwear, props my foot up on the bench, plants gentle kisses up my thighs. Her fingertips dance across my skin teasingly and it's both exquisite and frustrating - I want her fingers in me, her mouth on my clit, but I also don't want this gentleness from her to ever stop.

In the end it's not my choice, though, so I just enjoy it. She knows what she's doing, how to make me love this foreplay so much that I almost don't care that I'm pulsing with need, slick and ready for anything and anyone. But mostly ready for her.

Her fingertip traces my entrance. "Please," I whimper, and she finally gives it to me. First a finger, moving in and out so slowly I can hardly bear it.

Eventually a second, and she starts moving a bit faster.

After what feels like far too long there's a third, and a thumb on my clit, rubbing up and down every time her fingers fuck me. And the pleasure is building, the wave is coming, but it doesn't feel like enough. I want more.

Looking down at her, I see her watching me, the softest look on her face. My breath catches and my stomach explodes with butterflies. And I know what more I want, I don't just want to take. I want to give. I want something that equals that tender look, I want her to know that whatever she's feeling right now it's not just her, it's me too.

There's a flash of surprise on her face when I drop to my knees, but I don't see it for long, because I press my mouth against hers. The kiss is passionate, filled with meaning, and I hook my hands around her underwear, dragging it down. We don't break the kiss as she shifts to wriggle out of them, her fingers still working me from the inside and the outside both.

And when she throws aside the scrap of teal lace, I don't bury my fingers in her, but I shift so that I'm laying on my back on the shower floor. "Darce!" she laughs, but I just beckon her over. Water is running down her body as she straddles my face, so she laughs again and shakes her head, moving so that she's not directly under a showerhead, so that I won't drown while I'm licking her.

But I'm not paying attention to any of those practicalities, because all I want is to taste her. Now that we're not directly in the stream I wrap my arms around her thighs, pulling her down so that she's sitting on my face. There's a sigh, and the tension in her legs melts out of them. She shifts so that she's leaning over me, and I can't see what she's doing, but then suddenly the warm wet of her mouth is on me as well.

I'm not always into 69, but now I understand why Bex loves it. Giving and getting pleasure together, the push and pull, both at once. It doesn't feel distracting, but it feels like each part feeds the other, like the more I give the more I get. I know she's enjoying it because she's moving against me, riding my face as she attends to my pussy with her mouth.

I reach up with one hand and sneak a finger between her cheeks, brushing against her back entrance, and for a moment she freezes. Then, tentatively, she pushes back against my finger.

I want to be sure, so I pull away only far enough to ask "Yeah?" and she nods between my legs, so I push a little more firmly, breaching the first ring of muscle and her body opens up to let me in. There's a shaky breath against my pussy, and then she gets back to attending to me, licking and suckling and pumping her fingers in and out. She's riding my face in earnest again, and I take turns sucking on her clit and fucking her with my tongue, and my body starts tightening as hers does too, squeezing the finger that's in her ass, thighs that are acting as earmuffs tensing around me.

I want to make her come, want to come myself, want to make sure she knows how good this is, how much I'm enjoying myself, how this is pure bliss and every nerve in my body is activated, pulsating with pleasure.

And then it happens, I'm flung over the edge of my orgasm with a cry that echoes against the tile of the shower. She follows me a moment later, her thighs quivering. Quiet whimpers as her body moves weakly against mine, riding out the pleasure as she draws my own out with her mouth.

Then she collapses on top of me—warm, wet, slick skin against mine. I can tell it takes effort to heave herself off, both of us lying on our backs in the shower, and one of the guys reaches up to readjust the spray so that it's hitting us both.

I'd forgotten they were there, and when I glance over at their direction and they're sitting on the floor, backs against the wall, chests heaving from whatever it is that Bex and I missed because we were so wrapped up in each other. Alec's hand is on Rafael's knee, and Rafael's head is tilted back against the tile, eyes closed.

When my gaze meets Alec's he winks at me, and I give him a smile back, shifting a leg so that my foot nudges against his thigh. I feel like I ought to say something, but I don't want to break this spell that has settled in the shower. What happened between Bex and I feels weighty in a way that it hasn't before, and while I don't know what the guys did, something feels different there as well. And I want to just sit in it for a moment, in the pounding heart and fluttering stomach and tingling pussy.

A hand brushes against mine and it's Bex's. Our fingers weave together and I let my eyes close again, sinking into the silence.

I don't know how much time passes, but it's Rafael who speaks first.

"Well," he says, his voice gravelly. He clears his throat before trying again. "This shower is fucking huge."

I give a halfhearted chuckle, pushing myself up to sitting as Bex does the same. Her fingers drop mine as she moves next to Rafael, curling against his side, running the tip of her nose against his jawline. His arm slides around her waist and he pulls her closer, then she sighs and rests her head against his shoulder.

"I don't want to kill the vibe," Alec says. "And we don't have to do it right now, but I think we do need to talk. About where we go from here."

I nod, because he's right, it feels like something shifted. But I don't say anything, because I don't want to talk about it right now. Bex nods as well, but her eyes are still closed, which makes me think she feels the same. Rafael just turns his head and presses a kiss against the crown of Bex's head as silence settles over the shower again.

"Not now then," Alec says after a moment, and I shake my head. Glancing over at him he's studying me carefully, eyes probing in a way that makes me want to squirm. So I move towards him, straddling his lap and pulling my arms into my chest, then pressing myself against him. I rest my head on his shoulder, burying my face in his neck as his arms come up to wrap around my back. It's comfortable here, warm, but the fact that it's also close enough to escape his inquisitive eyes isn't an accident.

"Maybe the car ride back tomorrow," Bex says.

"Or we can do dinner together a week or two after we get back," says Rafael. "Give us some time to process as couples before we bring it to the group."

What he's saying makes sense, but also feels like he might be trying to pull away. Avoid it. I pull back and look at him.

"We're not going to get all awkward like we did last year, are we?" I ask, but he shakes his head. He meets my eyes and studies me for a long moment, and the way he's looking at me feels like something shifted there, too. Like something about the way we see each other is different, like our relationship has changed somehow. But before I can pinpoint it, he breaks eye contact and looks away.

"No, but a little time apart wouldn't hurt. If we're going to keep doing this, I think we need to be careful not to rush. There's no harm in going slowly."

The *if* in his statement isn't lost on me. Just a few days ago we'd talked about every year—they were the ones who brought it up. And now it's if? He's allowed to change his mind of course, we all are, at any time. But I thought changing minds would come from a discussion, not a declaration.

I don't verbalize any of this, because I don't know how to. Not in a way that's gentle and with the kind of sensitivity that this conversation deserves.

But I don't want this to be an if. I don't want to have this thing with Bex taken from me so suddenly.

What Alec has with Rafael.

What *we* have with *them*, really. This togetherness, this intimacy, this heat, the satisfaction, the tenderness. All of it.

But it doesn't feel like the right time to verbalize any of this. I feel like after whatever just happened I need to be very careful not to push, to let everyone process, individually and as married couples, so instead I just nod.

Rafael stands up and holds a hand out for Bex, pulling her to her feet and then wrapping a towel around her. Then he wraps one around himself, slung low on his waist, chest still damp from the shower. I admire them both, bodies that are hard in some places and soft in others, bodies that I never thought I would know as intimately as I now do.

"Y'all are hot," Alec says, mirroring my thoughts. Bex laughs and winks at him, pulling her towel apart to flash some thigh. Alec reaches out and catches her ankle, running his hand up her calf briefly before settling at her ankle again, and then kissing his fingertips with a flourish. "The legs on your wife," he says admiringly.

Rafael had been watching them with an unreadable expression, but his face flashes into a grin. "Your wife's tits though. They look like the perfect handful."

"They are," Alec says, reaching up to demonstrate, and when I look over at him he grins at me.

"Feeling a little objectified here," I say, and Bex laughs.

"I will comment on your husband's magnificent ass to make it even," she says.

"And your husband's arms are..." I fan myself, and she laughs again and nods knowingly.

"Now we're even," she says, and then leads Rafael out of the shower.

I don't make a move though, still sitting straddling Alec's lap, and tuck my face against his neck again, leaning into him. His arms come around me, hands tracing my back lightly as we sit in silence.

"You've got great legs too, you know," he says, and I chuckle against his skin.

"And your arms around me are my favorite thing in the world," I reply.

"Really? Your favorite?"

"Well, one of them."

"More than..." he doesn't finish his sentence, but instead nudges his pelvis against mine, and I laugh again.

"Well, I don't know about *more* than. But definitely perfect for after."

"Even if I wasn't involved in your before?"

I pull away to look at him, and he just looks back. "Yes," I say. "Are you still okay with that?"

He nods, then leans forward and presses a soft kiss to my mouth. "You?"

I nod, and he continues. "As we move forward—well, I guess *if* we move forward, things may change. Evolve. We should keep talking, checking in. Making sure we're still okay."

My mind flashes to the fact that there was more tenderness between Bex and I this week. Flashes to Alec playfully biting Bex's neck as he tried to convince us he was the alpha of the group. Flashes to the rough pad of Rafael's tongue against my palm before I gave Alec a hand job.

I push the thoughts away and nod.

"We should talk more about it when we get home," he adds, and I wonder what the *it* is for him, what memories and moments are flashing in his mind. If he's as unwilling to interrogate himself about whatever his *it* is as I am.

Then he gives my ass a light smack, and I follow his gesture to get up, nabbing towels for each of us. He takes his and instead of drying himself brings it up to my hair, rubbing it gently, and I just close my eyes and enjoy the attention. When he's done, he wraps it around my torso, and I wrap mine around his waist, dragging my fingers lightly up his happy trail to his belly button once I'm done, eliciting a soft sigh.

When we get back to the bedroom Bex and Rafael are already there, facing each other in bed and all tangled up, laughing quietly at whatever conversation they were having. We shed our towels and join them, Alec sliding in behind me and wrapping his arm around my waist as he pulls me against him.

"We had a lot of fun," Bex says after they turn to face us, Rafael spooning her as well.

"It wasn't too weird spending your anniversary watching your husband get his ass eaten out by another dude?" I tease.

"No—wait, what?" She turns to look at Rafael while Alec and I start laughing.

"It was in the bath while I was fucking you," Rafael says. "So you were probably distracted."

"Did you like it?" she asks.

Rafael looks a bit embarrassed and shrugs. "I mean... yeah. It feels pretty good."

"It does," she agrees, flushing, and then looks at me and covers her face in her hands. "I can't believe you convinced me to do butt stuff!"

"Hey, *you* asked *me*! I did zero pushing!" I insist. "Own it, Bex. You're really fucking hot, and you're doing incredibly sexy shit in bed. You blow your husband's mind on the regular, and now you make my toes curl occasionally."

"And mine!" Alec pipes in from behind me. "In a 'look but don't touch' sort of way, but still."

She takes a long look at me, and then another at Alec, and then rolls her eyes, but nods. "Yeah, okay. I'm pretty hot."

"Atta girl," Alec says, holding a hand up and she laughs and gives him a high five before snuggling back into Rafael's embrace.

But her voice is quiet and serious when she says, "There's no one else I'd do this with, you know. Y'all are the ones that I feel safe enough to play around with boundaries in this way."

Alec's arm wraps back around my midsection, tightening. It's true for me, too. I think this could have only ever happened with them.

I nod. "Same."

Chapter 18

THE CHECK-OUT TASK LIST for this place is pretty scant, which means that we can take the morning easy.

"They hire professional cleaners in between guests, so I guess they have them do everything," Rafael says. "Which makes sense, considering the clientele they cater to."

"Horned up orgies, you mean?" Alec asks, and Rafael nods with a grin.

I'm flipping through the guest book, reading the notes from the other guests that have stayed here. Some are the typical 'we had a great time' type of things you see in all guestbooks, but others are more sex-specific. One group of seven has tally marks next to everyone's name–an orgasm count, apparently. Others have profile handles and notes like *Look me up on Fetlife*, or *We're on Adult Friend Finder*.

"We should have tried having sex on the hammock!" I call out after one of the notes details how much fun they had doing just that.

"Ugh, I'm not coordinated enough, I'd end up on the ground," Bex says as she comes out of the kitchen with a mug and settles next to me on the couch.

"The grass can be fun too," I say, snagging the mug when she sets it down to steal a bit of coffee.

She glares playfully at me, but doesn't complain, instead nodding at the book. "You going to write something?"

"Yeah," I say, thinking for a bit longer before jotting down a note.

Husband and I came here with our best friends, and my pussy has never been more satisfied. The bathtub and the bed were my favorite spots, though the creek that's mentioned in the info folder is a very close third. Happy orgasms!

I've written the *D* of Darcy when Bex yelps, reaching for the pen. "Don't use your real name! What if someone we know sees it?"

"If someone we know is here, then they probably found it on the same website you did, so they have no room to talk."

She considers that for a moment, then shakes her head. "Just don't, please?"

I acquiesce, instead finishing the note with *DA+BR*. "Discrete enough?" and she nods, looking relieved. Then we pack up the car, hovering outside once we're done.

"I don't want to leave," Bex says, and I give her a tight smile, reaching out for her hand and pulling her towards me.

"It's not like we're never going to see each other again," I point out. "We live like a mile from each other."

"But it's different," she says, and she's right, though I wonder if it has to be. If there's a way to make whatever this is work. But instead of saying that, I just press a kiss to her mouth, and then a second, then a third. We pull back before we get carried away, and the guys finish up their goodbye kisses as well. Then we split up, Bex and Rafael in the front seat and me and Alec in the back.

The drive home goes by way too fast, and before I know it we're pulling into our driveway Rafael makes no move to turn off the car or get out.

"Are you guys good getting your stuff from the trunk? Catch up tomorrow?"

He's right. What would we do if they got out—just stand there awkwardly? I can't kiss Bex, or squeeze her hand. Even a lingering hug might look weird to other people. I'm not used to being this guarded around others—I've never shied away from PDA. This is going to take some getting used to.

I say as much when they pull away from our house, and Alec nods as he unlocks the front door, dropping our things in the entryway. "It feels way different from when we left last year."

"But also when we left last year that was supposed to be it. We weren't supposed to do this again. And don't get me wrong, I'm thrilled we did, but now we have to figure out how to navigate this, because it's going to be different."

After he closes the door behind us he turns to me, waiting patiently until I look back. "Are you catching feelings?"

There's no suspicion or anger or concern in his voice, it's neutral and his posture is open. But still, the question feels like a punch to my gut. I don't know how to answer that, but the fact that I don't know and the fact that the question affected me so much is telling me more than I want to admit. "I don't know. Sex and feelings haven't always gone hand in hand for me, but obviously it has since we got together. Maybe I'm out of practice with casual sex, and I forgot what it's like?"

"Maybe," he says, then focuses on his bag. I grab mine, following him up the stairs. "This is different than a one night stand, though. We've known them forever, already liked them. This is changing the kind of intimacy we have together, but it's not building it from scratch."

"Wait," I say, realizing. "Are *you* catching feelings?"

He glances back at me with a wry grin and shrugs before continuing to our bedroom.

"Is it just us, or do you think they are?" I press, and he shrugs again.

That's when it hits me. "That's why Rafael wanted to put off the conversation. Because they are too, and we need to have these conversations as couples before we have a big talk, all together."

"I think that's probably one of the reasons," he agrees.

My brain snags on the *one of*, and my heart jumps to my throat when I realize what another reason might be. In a very quiet voice, I say, "I noticed him more this time around."

He nods, but doesn't look at me, focused on getting our suitcases on the bed, and then opening his up. "I know."

Guilt bubbles in my gut, and there's a long, heavy silence.

"Is that-," I finally start, but he interrupts me.

"I did too. Notice her, I mean."

And I'm not mad or frustrated or jealous, because I get it. Because I think it's all of us. I am a little scared, though, and I step behind him, wrapping my arms around his waist and resting my head against his back. "We can figure this out," I say.

He nods, laying his arms against mine and tilting his head back so that it rests on mine.

Chapter 19

A FEW DAYS GO by before we talk about it again. It's the usual "catching up after vacation" busywork–Alec's work email exploded while he was out, our middle child, Melissa, had a fight with a friend, our youngest Kyle had questions about things he'd overheard at school, Jimmy had a major project due on Friday that he hadn't started. So we're busy with those things, exhausted by the time night time rolls around, and frankly don't want to start what is probably going to be a complicated conversation unless we know we have the energy to see it through.

It's not until the weekend comes that we find ourselves with time. Melissa is spending the night at a friend's, and Kyle and Jimmy are watching a movie on the couch downstairs. Alec is loading the dishwasher as I bring him things from the table, and when I'm done, I hoist myself up on the counter and watch him finish up.

"Hey," he says when he's done, stepping between my legs and resting a hand on either side of me.

"Hey yourself," I say after returning his kiss.

"You wanna?" he asks, nodding his head towards the stairs, and I laugh and nod, hopping off the counter and taking his hand as he tugs me in that direction.

"Heading upstairs!" he calls to the kids. "Go to sleep at a reasonable hour!"

Jimmy gives us a distracted nod, but Kyle yells, "Wait!" and jumps up to give us a goodnight hug and kiss before returning to the couch.

I lock the door once we're in our room, and when I turn around Alec is right there, crowding me against the wall. He kisses me once, then a second time, before pulling my shirt up and over my head and then tugging my joggers down my legs. I kick them off while working on his fly, then turn us around so that his back is against the wall, dropping to my knees and bringing his jeans down with me.

My hands slide up and down his thighs as I mouth him through his boxer-briefs, using more teeth than usual because he has the fabric protecting his sensitive skin. And when his head drops back against the wall with a thump I laugh, dragging his underwear down as well.

Taking him in hand, I lick the tip of his cock, tasting the salty precum that's gathered there. A swipe of my tongue around his crown to get things started, and then I wrap my lips around him. His hand fists my hair, the perfect amount of rough that tugs at my scalp and the small bite of pain that follows just heightens everything.

Alec's cock took some getting used to when we first got together, but after a decade and a half I've learned how to relax the back of my throat so that I can take him fully in my mouth. Looking up at him, he's watching me, finger tracing along my lips, around the mouth that's stretched wide open for him. I pull back and then slide up again, and this time his other hand joins the first, holding me gently in place, pulling me even deeper.

When I attempt to swallow he loosens his grip, but I don't move, instead reaching out for one of his hands and returning it to my hair. I see his chest rise and fall as he watches me, pulls me deeper, groans quietly as I successfully swallow around him.

When I start to pull back he releases me, and I swipe my tongue around his crown before going again, and then a third time. Then I lose count, and each time his grip on my hair gets tighter, the tug on my scalp shooting straight to my pussy. My eyes water, but the way he responds makes it all worth it, the moans, the look in his eyes, the way he touches my face gently when I've taken him as deep as possible.

Eventually I take his cock back in hand, pumping him slowly as I lick his balls, envelop them with my mouth, hum softly. He groans and breaks eye contact, head thumping against the wall again. A moment later, he hauls me up and grasps my hips, steering me backwards towards the bed.

When the backs of my knees hit the cover I fall back, and he shifts me so that I'm in the middle of the bed before settling on top of me. There's no talking, just touching and kissing and licking and grasping. I haven't removed my underwear, but it still feels good when he rubs against me, tongue tracing the shell of my ear and teeth scraping against my earlobe. And we do that for a bit, teasing with hands and mouths while we grind, waiting to see who gets impatient first and begins removing the final layer of clothes.

It's him, first tugging my bra down so that he has access to my breasts, then reaching behind me to unfasten it, and finally sliding his hand between us and replacing the pressure of his cock with his fingers as he rolls to his side. In return I slide my hand over him, grinning when he groans. He drops his forehead against my shoulder as he slips his hand under my underwear.

So I pull them down, kicking them off and spreading my legs so he can slide his fingers against me, pressure right where I need it.

"Fuck," he murmurs against my skin as I pump my hand along his length, and I just whimper in return, shifting against his fingers while he thrusts into my fist.

"Gonna need you inside me," I say a minute later, and when he slides a finger in I pull back and give him a playful look. "Not what I meant."

He smirks and adds a second finger.

"Your cock," I say, and while his third finger gets me closer to what I want, it's still not it.

"'Bout to swap you out for a toy," I tease, and that's when he finally pulls his hand away, positioning himself against my entrance and sliding home.

"That it?" he asks as he pulls out and pushes back in again, and I nod, breath catching when his pubic bone hits my clit with every thrust.

"Not bad," I manage to reply, and he throws his head back and laughs, grinding himself against me when he's buried deep in my pussy.

The friction makes me whimper, but when he asks, "How about that?" I just shrug. So he locks his legs around mine and rolls to his back, putting me on top. A smack to my ass and then he stretches out, resting his hands behind his head.

"You do the work, then," he says in a mock-annoyed tone, and I adjust myself, hands gripping the headboard so that I can fuck him from on top. It doesn't take long for his grin and laugh to fade, replaced by concentration in his forehead and quiet groans. One of his hands slips between us and fondles my clit as our rhythm increases, me sliding down on his length and him thrusting up from the bottom. The tension in me builds and his free hand grabs my hip and I can tell that he's getting close too, from the way that he grips me tighter and tighter.

"You close, baby?" he asks, and I nod, then lean all the way forward, pressing my mouth against his. He slides his lips open and our tongues tangle as we both get closer and closer and closer to our peak, his fingertips pressing against my skin as my thighs grip his sides.

"Fuck," I finally whimper, doing my best to keep the volume at a reasonable level as my body floods with pleasure. It's so good, so much, and he groans at the same time, a couple more thrusts until he's spent, though his fingers still rub my clit until *I'm* spent, on the way back down from my peak.

I collapse on top of him, resting my head on his chest and burying my face in his neck. My heart is pounding and I can feel his below me, also fast and strong, both our skin covered in a thin sheen of sweat.

A few minutes later, after I've regained enough energy to stand up and clean off, I return to the bedroom where he's drawn back the covers in our bed and crawled beneath the sheets. I join him, pressing my body against his for a post-coital cuddle, both of us still naked.

"We've still got it," he says as he covers us both with the comforter.

"Of *course* we've still got it," I say, and he chuckles quietly, looking down at me and pressing a brief kiss against my mouth.

"I wasn't actually worried," he says, and I believe him, because even though I wasn't actually worried either, I'm also a tiny bit relieved.

It's reassuring to know that we can go back to just being the two of us. That a vacation where we were intimate with different partners didn't mess up what we had. That we can still be fulfilled and satisfied and have really fucking amazing sex with each other, and just each other, without the novelty. That doing it on purpose this time didn't change anything once we got back.

We're quiet for a bit, just enjoying being skin against skin, feeling each other's breathing. Eventually he presses a kiss against my crown and rolls to his back and I shift, resting my head on his chest and draping my leg across his.

He reaches down and grasps my thigh lightly, thumb rubbing the skin there. "So what do we do?" he asks.

Even though I know what he's asking, I shrug, because I don't know the answer. "Do we do anything? What would doing anything even mean?"

"Not waiting a year or however long in between," he offers. "Seeing if they're up for doing this more often."

I nod, considering that. On one hand, there's no doubt that I'd love more time with Bex. More time just the two of us, behind closed doors. And not only for sex but also for the kind of physicality that would get us second glances from the outside world. Being able to hold her hand or get a lingering hug or drape an arm around her while we talk or watch tv or things like that–I want the casual intimacy I get with Alec with her, too.

But I also don't know if that's a good idea. If getting too attached could damage what Alec and I have. I know people do this, that polyamory exists and is a way people live their lives, but I don't know any of them personally. And I don't know if I could be one of them.

"You want to," I say, sidestepping the question, and this time he's the one that shrugs.

"I don't know," he admits. "Do I want more time with him? Yes. Do I think we should move forward with that..." he shrugs again instead of answering. "And if you're a no then I'm definitely a no. When it comes to Bex..."

My breath catches in my chest, because I'm even more nervous about this part.

"Don't worry," he says, probably reading my body language and the fact that I got completely still at the sound of her name. "Yes, I noticed her. In a way different than I did last year. But I don't know that I necessarily even want anything more than that. Right now even just admitting that I looked feels weird."

"Same," I say. "Both hearing you say that you looked and..." I pause, take a deep breath, continue, "admitting that I looked at Rafael too. Even if I'm not ready to actually act on the looking right now."

Alec raises his eyebrows. "You think you might be, though? Ready to act on it, at some point?"

"Shit!" I flush hot. "I didn't mean it like that... I don't know. I mean, maybe? But also maybe not. I really..."

"Don't know," he finishes for me, and I nod. "Do we know anything?" he asks with a halfhearted chuckle.

"That we're on the same page, it sounds like?" He nods at that. "That whatever happens we'll figure it out together?"

"No question," he says. "No matter what, we're a team."

We fall into silence again, and I trace patterns on his chest while I listen to his breathing, hear the kids come upstairs and get ready for bed.

"This is all still really weird," I say once their voices fade.

"What part's the weirdest?" he asks.

"Having a crush on someone I've seen naked, I think. Multiple crushes on multiple people I've seen naked. Other than you, I mean."

I glance up at him, and he's grinning. "You have a crush on me?" he asks, and I laugh.

"I mean, maybe a little one."

"Tiny?"

"Teeny tiny."

"Minuscule?"

"Almost non-existent."

He shimmies out from next to me, and shifts above me, holding himself up with his forearms and nudging his nose against mine. "Anything I can do to make you like me a little more?"

I grin, tracing the definition on his abs with my finger, then start down the happy trail, slowly. "I mean, you can try."

He presses a kiss to my collar bone before pushing himself up again. "I may not be very good."

"You'll probably be fine," I tease.

Another pushup, this time kissing the hollow of my throat on his way down. "I'll try my best."

"Partial credit for enthusiasm," I say, and I get a third kiss, this one on my other collar bone. "Also partial credit for whatever these pushups things are. The arm flex is really doing it for me."

He laughs and uses his arms to push himself further down, kissing one nipple, then the other, then the valley between them. I watch as he keeps moving, nipping at the skin of my chest and belly with his teeth, then tracing my stretch marks with his tongue, before he plants a kiss on each of the tops of my thighs.

"Put me in, coach," he says. "I promise to try my best."

With a mock-aggrieved sigh I spread my legs so that he has more room, bending my knees and resting my feet on either side of him. "I guess you can give it your best shot."

He laughs as everything but the top of his head disappears from view. A moment later his mouth begins its work, and I close my eyes, relaxing into the bliss.

Chapter 20

I'M NERVOUS WHEN WE walk into the gastropub that Rafael and Bex selected for our get-together a week later. Even just finding a place was harder than I expected–we wanted somewhere that we could have a conversation without being overheard, but didn't want a place with actual privacy. The idea of being alone with them feels a little loaded, even though I know that logically that's silly. It's not like we're horny teenagers who will pounce the moment the door closes.

But for whatever reason it seems like a good idea to avoid it.

They've snagged a booth in a corner, far enough from the soccer game playing at the bar that we'll be able to hear each other without yelling, but still benefiting from the background noise to give us some cover.

I'm probably overthinking things, but the feeling in my chest has only gotten tighter as today approached. Even walking in today Alec and I aren't entirely sure what we want. Well, the truth is that we probably *do* know what we want, but we're afraid to voice it: we want more time with them, more opportunities to be together, we want to figure out if there's anything to this beyond just great vacations. But opening that door would lead us to a dozen more questions, each one more complicated. So neither of us has actually said it.

"So," Rafael says after the waitress takes our orders. "Talking about this is somehow more awkward than doing it, but we're not going to be weird about it."

"Deal," I say with a halfhearted chuckle, and Alec nods as well. "Bex says you guys talked? Where did you land?"

They exchange a glance with each other, and Rafael nods at Bex, who takes a deep breath. "We–hopefully obviously–have a lot of fun with you guys. So we'd like to keep doing this, if you do."

"On vacation," Rafael tacks on quickly. "I–*we* think that's the best way to keep things from getting too complicated."

"How often?" Alec asks.

Rafael shrugs. "Once a year or so, I think. To keep from raising too many suspicions."

"Who do you think is going to get suspicious," Alec asks with a frown. "And what exactly do you think they'd suspect?"

Rafael shrugs again. "I don't know. People. The kids."

Alec's voice takes on a bit of an edge. "I don't think the kids are going to jump to 'they're taking more vacations together, they must be poly and fucking'."

"Of course not," Bex says, but Rafael cuts her off.

"We're not poly. Poly is relationships, this is just sex," he says, face impassive.

I don't know why hearing that hurts, but it does, and based on the stricken look that crosses Alec's face, I'm not the only one who finds it hurtful.

But Rafael is either unaware of how what he said hit us, or he's unwilling to acknowledge it. "Ethical non-monogamy, sure. Exclusive swinging, if such a thing exists."

Bex jumps in now, and from the way she's glancing at me I can tell that I'm not doing a good job hiding my feelings. "I mean, there's obviously a relationship, we're best friends. It's just not... romantic. It's like... grown-up, couple-friends with benefits."

I don't know if that softens the blow, or if I'm just hit with a wave of exhaustion that makes me care a little less. "Yeah," I say slowly, as Alec nods mutely next to me. "That makes sense. I told Alec that I think I'm out of practice with no-strings-attached sex, so this is a great chance to work that muscle again."

Bex's forehead wrinkles a bit, but she pastes a smile on her face. "Yeah, exactly."

Alec clears his throat. "Any rules or expectations between now and then? If Darcy and I find another couple we vibe with... is that okay? Since this isn't a relationship?"

Alec and I hadn't discussed this, and when I glance over at him his face is harder than I expected. A flash of hurt crosses Rafael's, and Bex nods, a little hesitantly.

"I mean... we can't control what you do on your own time. Nor do we want to. I think, if that happens, we'd want to know?" She turns to her husband, who nods but I can see a muscle twitching in his jaw. "Yeah," she continues. "We'd want to know, if you were comfortable telling us. And we'd figure out what that means when it happens."

"*If* it happens," I say, glancing at Alec. Because I don't *want* to find another couple to vibe with, I just want Bex and Rafael. "We can cross that bridge if we come to it."

"So we'll talk again next summer?" Alec asks, and it takes all my self control not to roll my eyes.

I do my best to send him *'you're being a child'* telepathically, and then say out loud, "I mean, obviously the friendship part of this," I gesture between the four of us, "won't change. We're still going to be talking and hanging out and texting during band concerts. Just not... you know. Fucking."

"Right!" Bex says, her voice overly cheerful.

A loud cheer comes from the bar—Austin FC has apparently just scored a goal—and Rafael stands up. "Going to go check out the game," he says.

Once he's gone, Bex looks at us, a little apologetically. "I'm sorry. He's just—"

But Alec cuts her off, standing up as well. "Gotta take a piss," he says, stalking off towards the bathroom.

I actually do roll my eyes once he's disappeared from view, then look at Bex. "Our husbands are children."

She chuckles halfheartedly. "I think this has been really weird for Rafe. I mean, a year ago he wasn't even out, and now he's..."

"Negotiating bisexual orgies in the middle of restaurants," I say, and this time her laugh is real.

"Exactly. And this year it's not just the physical stuff between him and Alec, it's also..." She swallows, "Other stuff."

I nod, thinking about the *other stuff* that Alec and I have discussed. Wondering if they've discussed similar, and that's why Rafael seemed so defensive, was so insistent that this was just sex. "Since last year, things have kind of..." I pause, trying to find the right word, one that dances around the issue closely enough without actually spelling it out. Because telling her that my feelings are developing feels too vulnerable, and it's not my place to tell her about Alec's. "... progressed, I guess."

There's a flash of relief on Bex's face as she nods, her hand flying out in agreement. "Yes, that. Things... progressed for us too. And it's weird for both of us, but I think he's struggling a little more than I am."

I want to ask her exactly what they talked about. I want to know if they're catching feelings, if she finds herself thinking about me in a daydreamy way sometimes. If once a year really feels like enough, or if she wishes there was a way for more, to integrate pieces of it into our usual lives. If the line between platonic and romantic is becoming blurry.

And I want to know how she's feeling about Alec. If her stomach fluttered when Alec ran his hand down her calf, or when he bit her on the shoulder. If she replays those moments as often as I replay Rafael's tongue on my palm. If she's mentioned noticing Alec, or if Rafael noticed mentioning me. If he noticed me noticing him.

God, it's like I'm a teenager again. I'm being ridiculous. I might as well pass her a note to pass to her husband. *Do you really like my tits, or were you just being polite since Alec complimented Bex?*

"What?" she asks, pulling me away from my thoughts, and even though blushing isn't my norm, my face flushes a little warm.

"Nothing."

She calls my bluff by raising her eyebrows but otherwise not saying anything, so I shrug.

"I'm just thinking about... the progression. And how it makes me feel like a bumbling awkward teenager sometimes. And I don't like that at the age of thirty-nine, I thought I was past it."

"Yeah," Bex says quietly, and our eyes meet. I'm caught in her gaze for a moment, and she seems caught in mine, the air heavy with things unsaid.

Both of us holding back not only out of respect for our own marriages, but for each other's marriages.

We're not there, but part of me hopes we will be, one day. That there's a *yet* at the end of *we're not there.*

"Anyway," she says, clearing her throat and looking away. "None of us imagined that this was going to be a chapter in our marriages."

"Do you think things will be weird between them for long?"

She shrugs, then shakes her head. "No. You and I are good, right?"

I nod, relieved, because I have no idea what I'd do if things weren't.

"Then they'll be fine. They just need some time."

***

When the guys eventually return, Bex and I do our best to carry the conversation and keep things as light as possible. The guys play along as best they can, and even though it only half works it feels like progress.

Javi apparently *also* waited until the last minute to do his social studies diorama. Their middle daughter, Ximena, wants to play soccer again in the fall and begged Rafael to coach. We promise to ask Melissa if she wants to play as well, and Bex tells Alec that Rafael is going to recruit him as assistant coach if she does. Kyle wants their youngest, Simon, to spend the night, but Simon hasn't spent the night with anyone but his grandparents.

"He's my baby!" Bex says, clasping her hands over her heart. "I'm not ready for sleepovers!"

"We promise to take good care of your baby," I tell Bex, and she nods.

"I know, and you guys make perfect sense as the first one anyway. We'll look at the calendar."

By the time dinner is eaten and dessert is shared, things are starting to feel like normal. And with time things will be better, I tell myself. If we could recover from the weirdness of last time, we can recover from this.

Rafael clearing his throat pulls my attention back to the table.

"I hope you know," he says, and he's looking straight at Alec as he speaks, so there's little doubt that this message is for him. "It's not about being queer. I haven't really come out because who the fuck cares that a thirty-eight year old dude who's married to a woman just realized he's bi. But my hesitation about people knowing about all this has nothing to do with the fact that you're a dude. It's because I'm married."

I rest my hand on Alec's thigh and he covers it with his, squeezing my fingers. That particular concern hadn't even occurred to me, but apparently it had crossed Alec's mind, and I feel some of the tension leave his body.

"Thanks," Alec says, his voice quiet, and Rafael just nods.

"And for the record," I say, and Rafael directs his attention at me. "*We* give a fuck. You're not obligated to come out to anyone if you don't want to, but we care. And we'd care even if you weren't hooking up with Alec, even if you guys were monogamous and had no plans to change that. You're our friend, and anything that's important to you is important to us. I hope you know that."

Rafael nods, and Bex presses a kiss to his shoulder, then leans her head against it.

"And before we leave..." I fish a flash drive out of my purse and slide it across the table to them. "Your anniversary gift. If you want, I can invite you to the app we use and we can send you the copies for your phones as well."

"That'd be great," Bex says, and when she reaches for it our fingers brush. She gives me a small but genuine smile, and I try to ignore the fact that my skin tingles with the ghost of her touch.

I send them the invites to the app and create a group that's shared between the four of us, copying the pictures from the group that Alec and I share privately. "They're pretty big files so it'll take a bit for them to copy," I tell them. "But you'll get a notification when it's done."

"Thanks," Bex says, reaching across the table and giving my arm a squeeze. "For everything."

I can tell she means it, that it's not overacting to make things seem normal, but it's sincerity. And between that and Rafael's confession and Alec's acceptance of it, we might be heading in the right direction. On the way to being whatever it is that we're supposed to be in between our vacations.

"Of course," I say sincerely. "Anything for our besties."

Part Two

July

rafe

When I first started my job, I didn't have many business trips—I was too junior for that. But as I've moved up in the chain, they've become more and more common, and at this point they're practically monthly. And while I don't mind the occasional one, regular business trips aren't my thing.

"I'm going to miss you," Bex says, draped across the bed that my suitcase is lying on, watching me pack.

"I'm going to miss you too," I say, stretching over her in order to give her a quick kiss.

She grabs my ass and pulls me against her, rubbing her clothed pussy against my clothed dick, and I laugh, struggling to escape her grip.

"Not now, I have to pack!" I protest, but she shakes her head, locking her legs around my thighs and trying to pull me further down.

"You can pack after!"

"After what?" I ask. She wiggles her eyebrows and I decide to stop struggling, falling heavily against her, and when my body presses her into the bed she gives a content sigh.

"Mmmmm. My favorite."

"This?" I ask, burying my face in her hair, which is spread out against the covers. "I'm not even doing anything."

"This," she agrees, and I can feel her softening against me, hands coming up to drag along my back. It's enough to make me want to pull my shirt off so that I can feel her fingertips against my skin, featherlight along my spine. "Your weight on me, us pressed up against each other completely."

"It's nice," I agree, trying to remember why I'd protested this a minute ago. I can pack later--she's not taking me to the airport until after we drop the kids off their summer camp in the morning.

Convinced, I reach under the hem of her shirt, skimming my hands up along her sides.

"What're you doing?" she asks, and I can hear the smile in her voice, the victory.

"Nothing," I reply, pushing up with one forearm so that I can see as I reveal her skin--first her waist, then her stomach, then her bra-covered tits. She pushes herself up and helps me toss the removed item of clothing somewhere on the floor, then hooks her thumbs under the waistband of her yoga pants, shimmying out of both them and her underwear in just a few seconds.

"In a hurry?" I ask as her hands go for the fly of my slacks, and she grins up at me.

"Trying to get you in me before you change your mind and decide to pack."

"As if I could ever turn down this," I say, gesturing to her and then leaning down to nip at the bump in her bra, a nipple that's already pebbled under the fabric.

"Not gonna risk it," she says, but once the button and the zipper of my pants are undone I don't help her remove them, too busy mouthing her through the fabric. She stops attempting to undress me after a moment, instead relaxing against the bed as I give her breasts all the attention they deserve, then slide one hand down between her legs.

Once I've slipped past her curls and her folds, I pull back, looking at her in surprise.

"How are you already this wet?"

She shrugs. "I was thinking sexy things while you were doing the dishes."

"Doing the dishes turns you on?"

"*You* doing the dishes turns me on," she says, spreading her legs a little further. "It's super hot."

"What were you thinking?" I ask, brushing a finger against her clit, and she sighs, eyes falling shut. I lightly rub her, dipping my mouth close to her ear. "What was going through that mind of yours that got you all slick for me?"

She just hums contentedly in response, so I pull my hand away, and her eyes fly open. "What?"

"If you want my hand," I say, brushing a finger against her again. "You need to tell me what you were thinking of."

"This," she says, shifting against my touch. "You. Over me, touching me, inside me. Hands gripping, cock pumping, muttering in Spanish."

"I don't mutter in Spanish."

"You do," she argues, eyes flashing seductively. "And it's very hot. It got me wet just thinking about it."

"Nice." I say. "Anyone else in that fantasy of yours?" Sometimes the answer is yes, and that gets me going too, her telling me about Darcy sitting on her face while I fuck her, or me fucking her mouth while Darcy eats her out.

But today her face gets soft and she shakes her head, looking at me seriously. "Tonight it's just you."

Even though everything we do with Alec and Darcy is red hot, and I have no issue with them sometimes showing up in our dirty talk–we both invite them in at times–her answer tonight is exactly what I need. That at this moment, just me is enough.

"It's just you for me too, tonight," I say, and the smile that creeps across her face gives my heart a squeeze. Because this is the woman I fell in love with, married, had three babies with, am building a life with. And I love her more than I can stand.

Dipping my head down, I whisper into her ear, palm rubbing her clit as my middle finger traces her opening. "Just me and my good girl. That's all I need tonight."

My finger slips inside her at the end of that sentence, and she makes a soft sound, though I don't know if it's because of that, or because of how much she loves being called a good girl. I pull my finger out and when I slide it in again another whoosh of air escapes, eyes fluttering shut. My thumb draws circles on her clit as my middle finger strokes her from the inside, and for a few minutes the room is quiet except for the sounds of us breathing.

Eventually I add a second finger and her eyes open lazily, gaze focusing slowly on me. "Getting me ready for the main event?" she asks, and I shrug.

"Can do this for as long as you want," I say, then squint at her phone, which is plugged in on her nightstand. "Well, we have to get the kids up in eight hours, so I can do it for seven and a half. Still need to pack."

"Oh, God, I'd be a boneless pile of goo after seven and a half hours of this," she says, and I laugh.

"I, on the other hand, would definitely *not* be boneless," I counter. "But I'd still do it."

"You would," she agrees, reaching down to attempt removing my pants once again. "But tonight I want your dick."

This time I help her, shucking my pants off one handed, but removing my fingers from inside her so I can pull my shirt up and over my head. She's looking at me with admiring eyes when I'm done, hot gaze trailing down my body. Once she's at my cock she reaches out for it, and I bite back a groan as her fingers wrap around me, giving me a light squeeze. Bex wraps her other hand around the back of my neck and tugs me back down to her, positioning me at her entrance as my body settles against hers again.

"Fuck me?"

She asks it as if she's not sure of the answer, as if there's anywhere on earth I'd rather be than here, tip of my cock pressed against her. Bex spreads her legs further, shifting down a fraction of an inch, and she's so wet for me that I slide in that fraction, surrounded by wet heat.

"Of course," I say, pushing myself up on my forearms and thrusting the rest of the way.

The noise she makes is oh so quiet, but rough and primal and she pulls back when I pull out, shifting her hips forward when I thrust, meeting me halfway. Another noise, and I love her noises, the way they're only loud enough for me to hear. I tuck every one away to the same private corner of my mind where I keep the way she looks when she comes, the feel of her spasming around my fingers when I hit her g-spot, the way she tastes when I lick her to ecstasy. She's imprinted on every one of my senses.

We continue moving against each other, developing a rhythm, and with one hand I pull the cup of her bra down, capture a nipple between my lips. I suck and lick as her breath speeds up, pulling away to scrape my teeth against her skin, attempt to leave a small hickey on the underside of her breast. Then I free her other tit and give it the same treatment, all while I pump in and out of her.

But soon I have to stop the additional attention, instead reaching down between us to get her to the peak that I'm rapidly approaching. "I'm close," she pants, wrapping one leg up and around my ass, using that leverage to slam into me with as much force as I'm plunging into her. "Fuck, Rafe, it's so good."

"*You're* so good, mi vida," I tell her. Because she *is* that, she's my life, my everything, and nothing and no one can change that. She's all I need, and is more than enough, and I don't know how to put those feelings and thoughts into words, so I try to put them into sex, into this physical expression of our relationship. I need her to know that living a life with her and no one else would be bliss, would be beyond what I dreamed of as a twenty-two year-old college senior, taking her on her first date, almost two decades ago.

"I'm gonna," she warns me, and I respond with what feels like a weak expression of everything I'm feeling for her.

"I love you."

"I—" But she doesn't finish what she was going to say, instead arching against me suddenly. A couple more pumps and I follow her over the edge, thankful that all thinking disappears and all I know is here and me, overcome by the bliss of what we can do together.

***

The next morning, after day camp drop off, we drive to the airport.

"Buy extra batteries for the vibrator?" I ask, and she laughs, reaching out to lace her fingers with mine.

"Of course. Makes the time go faster while you're gone."

"If you ever want to record one of those sessions..."

She rolls her eyes, bumping her elbow against mine. "And risk Javi coming across that video when he's stolen my phone to Facetime a friend? Not likely."

I glance at her, wiggling my eyebrows. "The app though..."

"Oh!"

She pauses, and after a moment I cut into the silence. "No pressure, I'm mostly just teasing anyway. I mean, I'd love a sext, but not if you feel weird about it."

"You know I've always been a little paranoid about the kids seeing it or it getting mixed into other family pictures and showing up on the electronic picture frame or something. But you're right, the app fixes that concern."

She pulls up to the airport curb, putting the car in park, and then looks at me with a mischievous little grin. "Maybe it's time."

I can't help but grin back, leaning forward to capture her mouth with mine. "I would be most honored to receive anything you sent."

"Will you send something back?"

"You want a dick pick?"

She shrugs, but her grin hasn't changed. "If it's your dick? And you're holding it, like you're about to get yourself off while you think of me? Yeah, absolutely."

"Maybe I will," I say flirtatiously, and when she licks her lips I decide I need to get out of the car before I develop a hard-on in the middle of the drop-off lane at the airport.

I gather her in one more hug and one more quick kiss, and then head inside.

***

The flight to Los Angeles is a quick two and a half hours, and when I arrive I go straight into the office, busy with meetings, followed by a happy hour and dinner with colleagues I haven't seen since my last trip. Facetiming the kids before bed generally isn't possible on the first day of my trip, though I'll be able to do it one or two times while I'm gone.

While I'm at dinner my phone vibrates, and the notification says that it's from the app. I briefly consider ducking into the bathroom to check it, but she deserves my undivided attention, so instead I shoot off a quick text.

At dinner so I can't check it, but I absolutely will when I get back to the hotel. Love you, and can't wait!

Her reply is just an embarrassed emoji. I must look like I'm up to something because a colleague makes a crack about the look on my face, so I silence my phone and stuff it back into my pocket, intent on ignoring it for the rest of the evening.

I don't get back into the hotel until midnight, so with the time change there's no doubt that Bex is asleep. But I still peel off all my clothes, grab a hand towel, and crawl into the hotel bed, prepared to send back a picture that she'll get when she wakes up in the morning.

I enter the passcode to the app, and when it opens there's a picture of Bex laying on our bed, holding the phone above her head with her full body visible. She's wearing a strappy black lace teddy that's sheer enough that I can make out every curve of her body, and even with how exhausted I am, I feel my cock start to wake up. The message below it reads:

> *As requested. The bed is lonely without you, but I'll find a way to keep myself occupied tonight. Can't wait until Friday, but in the meantime feel free to rub one out while thinking of me.*

That will *not* be a problem. I take my cock in hand, noticing there are other messages below that one, so I keep scrolling.

> *Darcy: I'll only rub one out while thinking of you because you asked so politely.*

What the fuck?

Bex: DARCY?!

Bex: Wait, what happened?

Bex: Rafe is out of town, this was supposed to be for him!

Darcy: We figured. The folder where I sent the pictures has all four of us, if you want to send something for just the two of you, you need to create a new one.

Bex: Alec's here too?

Alec: [forrestgumpwaving.gif]

Bex: [jimhidinginhiscar.gif]

Darcy: [taylorblowingkisses.gif]

Darcy: Okay, we'll leave you alone now. If you can't figure out how to make a new folder, lmk and I'll talk you through it tomorrow.

Bex: ugh. ty

Alec: Enjoy rubbing one out, R!

Just thinking about Bex's embarrassment has my cock deflating, and I rest my head in my hands, though I can't help but laugh. Because of *course* the first time she sends me nude pictures, it's intercepted by friends. At least it's Darcy and Alec, who have already seen her naked. And while things are still a bit awkward, the past month has done a good job of putting enough distance between us and the last trip that Alec and I are handling the friendship a bit better. While we haven't hung out one-on-one, we're texting like normal, and we'll be coaching our daughters' soccer team in the fall together as well.

There's a red notification dot on the folders icon, and when I hit it I realize Bex created a new folder. This one is just for the two of us

Bex: OMG I'M SO EMBARRASSED

Bex: I mean, it should be fine, they've seen me naked before so it's no big deal, right?

Bex: BUT IT'S STILL REALLY EMBARRASSING.

Bex: FUCK FUCK FUCK

Bex: I'm fine, it's fine, this is no big deal.

Bex: Don't worry about me, by the time I wake up tomorrow I'll be feeling less humiliated.

Bex: Call me when you wake up, though, just to make sure I'm not spending the day hiding in bed.

Bex: AND I'M STILL EXPECTING THAT DICK PIC!

Her still demanding a dick pic seems like a good sign, and I guess after everything she's gone through tonight it's the least I can do.

It takes me a minute to get back in the mind frame, and I resist the urge to pull up some porn, instead playing back a reel of my and Bex's greatest hits. Eventually I'm back there and I lean back in the bed, shooting a picture from thighs up, cock in hand.

And once that's done I flip to the pictures of us fucking that Alec took on our last trip. Bex was so fucking hot that day and knowing Darcy and

Alec were there too made it even hotter. Having them watch as I eat her out, finger her g-spot, fuck her until she came, is such a power trip. We're great together, but I'm not about to brag about that to anyone. But it turns out fucking in front of people is more than bragging, it's us putting our money where our mouth is and *showing* them.

As I approach my peak I imagine her here, next to me, tickling my balls and kissing me as my hand moves faster and faster. Sometimes we do just that, make out while masturbating to mix things up. I can easily picture us doing it now, knowing that next up would be her turn, and I'd get to watch her hand at work on her clit, her tits raise and lower with each breath. How sometimes she gets so wet that you can hear it, the sound of her rubbing layered on top of everything else that's happening. Watching her get herself off is so fucking hot, and almost always makes me want to fuck afterwards, though if I've already come once that night it's not necessarily possible.

The tension in my body increases, and my heart is racing, breath quick. I know it's coming but still am almost caught off guard as my body clenches, then releases. Overwhelming pleasure spreads through my body and I slow my hand but keep it going to draw out another few moments as the sensations shudder through me for a bit longer.

And then I lay there, limp and spent. Once I've gathered the energy, I wipe myself off with the towel and then grab my phone to send Bex a message.

Fuck, that was good. Imagined you were here and next up.
Looking forward to doing it for real on Friday.

Then I flip to the conversation with the four of us.

I missed all the fun, damn California time!
Well, I didn't miss ALL the fun. (And thanks for the
good wishes, A, I did enjoy it.)

I drag myself out of bed and head to the bathroom, turning on the shower and getting in to rinse off once the water's warm.

I remember after we fucked for the camera, we collapsed on the bed, and after a moment Bex giggled quietly and pointed at Darcy. She was spread out on her back, one hand still in her pants, with an unmistakable post-orgasm flush.

Bex and Darcy don't really look alike, Bex with dark hair and more of a 'girl next door' fresh-faced appearance while Darcy is more of a blonde bombshell. Bex is definitely more my type, but I can't deny that Darcy's gorgeous as well. She's hard to ignore. And having a gorgeous woman hump her hand while she watches you fuck your wife is a huge ego boost. Because even though I didn't *actually* make her come, I did have a part in two beautiful women's orgasms that night, which is a real trip.

I hadn't even realized that my hand had drifted down to my cock, stroking it lightly again as I thought about that night and Darcy, but when I do, I stop and pull it away. Because even though Bex and I have talked about this, about how her eyes wandered to Alec more this past trip and I found myself thinking about Darcy more than I had the first time, it still feels wrong. It's why when we met to discuss our arrangement I thought a clean break would be good.

Well, that and the fact that I'm feeling things for Alec that I wasn't expecting. Bex is too, for Darcy, but that doesn't bother me nearly as much as my own feelings. I trust her, but for whatever reason I don't trust myself.

I shouldn't have taken the bait, sent that message to Alec. It's not fair of me to flirt but refuse anything else, and there can't *be* anything else, regardless of where my mind drifts when I'm not paying attention. Tonight, in my post-orgasm haze I just wasn't thinking, but I need to do a better job of guarding my thoughts.

Once I'm out of the shower I dry myself off and pull on some underwear before getting back in bed. I pull out my phone for one more text to Bex before I fall asleep.

Love you. Talk tomorrow.

***

The time change always works in my favor on business trip mornings, and even though I wake up at seven, it feels like I've slept in. There's a message from Bex in our regular text chain, reminding me she has an appointment this morning so she'll call when she's done, and a notification from the app as well. When I flip to it, it's in our group chat, two messages from Darcy after my last one, about an hour apart.

Darcy: [tellmemore.gif]
Darcy: Sorry, didn't mean to go against our agreement. I'll

let you two discuss the dirty details amongst yourselves. Hope
everyone has a great day! [taylorhearthands.gif]

With a groan I drag myself out of bed. Because she's right, flirty texts go against what we agreed on. I should have known better than to open the door.. That was the whole point was to return to what our friendship used to be like between trips, and telling your best friends that you just masturbated isn't that. But it also *felt* so normal. Shifting back to how things were before this most recent vacation is going to be harder than I thought. But anything other than back to the way things were just isn't feasible. With more than that there's the danger of getting lost in the lust of it all, of it affecting our primary relationships, of getting sloppy and accidentally revealing ourselves to people that would judge us or our kids for it.

Bex video calls while I'm getting ready for the day, and I sit on the bed. She's on our living room couch, a sheepish look on her face.

"Feeling better?" I ask.

She nods. "Yeah, it's whatever. Nothing they haven't seen before, I guess. And at least it was a good picture."

"It was a fucking *amazing* picture, mi vida. Bet Darcy is going to pull that out at least once between now and our next trip together."

She blushes but laughs, fluttering her eyelashes at the camera coyly. "Who could blame her?" she teases. "You got a little flirty there, wasn't expecting that."

I grimace a little. "Was in post-orgasmic bliss and not thinking, sorry about that."

"It's fine," she insists. When we talked about it after our vacation, Bex was more on board with us having an honest conversation with them about everything–I was the one that held back. Her eyes shift away from the phone camera, instead focusing on something on the wall behind it. "Darcy's apology was interesting."

"Yeah?"

"Just in terms of... I don't know. Whether or not that was going against our agreement."

She's still not looking at me, so I pick up my hand and wave it at her to draw her attention. "What aren't you saying?"

Bex lets out a long breath, then looks at me. "If we... I don't know. Kept that group chat going. Would that be too line-blurry for you? If it is, then that's fine, I'm totally on board with not. Please don't see this as me pressuring you, because I–"

I cut her off. "I know you're not pressuring me. I hadn't really thought about it, I guess. It doesn't seem as... dangerous isn't the right word."

"Tempting fate?" she supplies, and I nod.

"I mean, it's just text." It could be a way to expel some of that tension so that in person interactions are less loaded. It took us a while to really get back to normal last year, and especially after the dinner we had, I don't want that this year. And honestly I know we can't return to life pre-hooking up, much as sometimes I'd want to.

And sometimes I *don't* want to, I want to go the other direction, which is a whole other level of complicated feelings that I'm not going to excavate today.

"What do you think?" I ask.

"I'm only fine with it if you're one hundred percent on board," she says, and I know that she's being honest. If I said no, she'd go along with it. We've both agreed that this is our approach to this friends with benefits situation we have with them. "Think about it," she adds. "Whatever you decide, I'm good."

I nod, and then we shift into conversations about the kids and the meetings I have coming up today. And before I know it, time is up, and I need to finish getting ready and head in to work.

***

When I'm in our L.A. office I generally share a conference room with someone else who's here for the week, and in between meetings I flip back to the thread between the four of us. Taking a deep breath, I type out a message.

> *Bex and I have talked about it, and we're down with texting if y'all are.*

I leave my phone in my bag for the next meeting, because knowing there's a notification and not being able to check it would be too distracting. And when I get back from the meeting, there's a reply.

> *Alec: Yeah? We're down. What are the guidelines, what goes, what's off limits?*

There's also a private text from Bex.

> *Bex: Your call, whatever you're comfortable with, I am.*

I think for a minute before replying to the group.

Rafael: Text and pictures are good. Let's see what happens and go from there?

Darcy: Sweeeeeeeet. How do you feel about gifs?

Bex: Like sex gifs?

Darcy: [eiffeltower.gif]

Rafael: Gifs are fine, but I'm at work!

Darcy: Probably shouldn't check this thread at work then!
Darcy: Posting more in 5...4...3...2...

Rafael: [middlefinger.gif]

I close the app, change the notifications from it to silent, and then switch to my normal text thread with Bex.

Rafe: Meetings till 5, but I can Facetime with the kids tonight?

Bex: Perfect. Love you, talk then!

There's a notification from the app, but I tell myself I'm not allowed to open it until after work. It'll be a treat at the end of the day, and I'm sure that whatever gifs Darcy is spamming it with will make it worthwhile.

My colleague sticks his head through the conference room door. "Meeting's up. Hey, what's got you grinning?"

"Just some friends," I say. "Being ridiculous."

"Best kind of friends," he says with a laugh, and I nod.

"These definitely are."

August

text messages

Darcy: Truth or dare

Rafael: I'm sorry, did we time warp back to high school and I missed it?

Darcy: Oh, good, Rafael has volunteered to go first! Truth or dare, Rafael.

Rafael: [rolleyes.gif]
Rafael: Truth, I guess.

Darcy: What did you do last time you started feeling horny at work?

Rafael: Last time? Ignored it and focused on whatever I was supposed to be working on.

Alec: Wait, does the answer change if we're not talking about last time?

Rafael: Are you asking if I've ever jacked off at work?

Darcy: [RuddAbsolutely.gif]

Rafael: [shrug.gif]

Bex: (Yes, yes he has.)

Rafael: BEX!

Bex: That's what happens when you leave the state and aren't around to take my phone away. I tell all your secrets!

Darcy: Gonna need the details.

Rafael: I mean, who hasn't gotten off at work?

Darcy: [raiseshand.gif]

Bex: [raiseshand.gif]

Rafael: Bex, you're lying, because I've gotten you off at work before.

Bex: Your work, not mine. Totally different.

Alec: When did you have sex at work?

Rafael: It was a while ago, before open workspace offices became trendy.

Darcy: Bex, truth or dare.

Rafael: Didn't you just go? Isn't it my turn now?

Darcy: Fine

Rafael: Bex, truth or dare.

Bex: WHY ME?

Rafael: Because you told everyone I jack off at work.

Bex: Truth, I guess.

Rafael: Biggest unfulfilled fantasy.

Bex: Orgy with my husband and our best friends.
Bex: Oh, wait, you said unfulfilled! Ummmm, hot masseuse that gets a little handsy.

Alec: Do they just get you off, or do you guys fuck?

Bex: Depends on my mood when I'm daydreaming. Sometimes it's all about me, sometimes it isn't.

Darcy: Did you go into the massage looking for it?

Bex: Oh, definitely not. But they start rubbing my glutes or my upper thighs and...

Rafael: [takingnotes.gif]

Darcy: How long are you in Cali this time?

Bex: Three more days
Bex: [crying.gif]

Alec: Ouch.

Darcy: Hey babe, want to come to give me a massage?

Alec: Sure, I'll be right there.

Bex: I hate you.

Darcy: No you don't
Darcy: [blowingkisses.gif]

September

alec

"THANK YOU FOR PLAYING hooky with me today," Darcy says as she pops a piece of popcorn into her mouth. "I'll make sure to make it worth your while when we get home."

I grin at her, then gesture to the empty theater. "Looks like it's just going to be us, so maybe you won't have to wait until we get home."

She laughs, and as she leans over to give me a kiss she grips my upper thigh with her hand, giving it a little squeeze. I try not to groan into her mouth, because even if the theater's empty, we're in public, and there's probably someone in the projection booth as well.

But when the theater darkens a few minutes later she pulls away, because my wife always insists on watching the trailers. And that's when we realize another couple came in while we were making out, the backs of their heads silhouetted against the screen. This time I *do* groan, but it's an unhappy one, and Darcy laughs quietly next to me.

"Guess we have to be on our best behavior," she whispers in my ear, and her breath tickles the hairs on my neck. "If you're good, you'll get to pick where and how I get you off afterwards."

I turn to look at her, capturing her mouth with mine and slipping my tongue past her lips for a kiss before the movie starts.

"Fuck yes, I will."

***

I spend most of the movie trying to pay attention to what's happening on the screen, as opposed to Darcy's hand on my thigh, occasionally sneaking up and brushing against my crotch. I'd feel bad about occasionally copping a feel myself since we're in public, but the couple that's a few rows ahead of us does their own share of making out as well.

You'd think that almost a decade and a half into our relationship we might not spend the afternoon teasing each other with sly glances and brief touches, but after a bit of a dry spell when our youngest was born, we've rediscovered our sexual groove. When the lights come up, I'm just as ready to get her under me as I was when she invited herself up to my place on our first date.

I'm following Darcy's tug down the aisle when I realize that I know the other couple that was in the theater with us. "Art! Guess I'm not the only one playing hooky from work, you and Claud–"

I cut myself short when I realize the woman with him isn't his wife Claudia.

Art clears his throat, nodding to the woman next to him. "Alec, hey. This is Jen. Jen, this is my colleague Alec and his wife Darcy."

"Hi," Darcy says, a big smile pasted on her face. We shake hands, and then Art and Jen excuse themselves, making their way out of the theater quickly.

"They were..." I start, trying to make sure I was remembering correctly. Because they *were* kissing during the movie, I'm sure of it. But he and

Claudia have been together as long as I've known him, and they have two teenagers together.

"They were," Darcy says, threading her fingers with mine and tugging me down the aisle again. "Maybe they have an open relationship."

Again, I stop. Because Darcy's right, even though my mind went straight to judgment. The assumption that he was cheating on her. Which is pretty ironic considering I semi-regularly flirt via text with a married man who's blown me before and with any luck will do it again. "Why didn't I think of that?"

She shrugs, planting both feet and yanking on my arm. "Because it's not what you default to yet. Come *on*."

I follow her out of the theater and into the car. "Why do you default to that?"

"Probably because I joined a Facebook group for non-monogamous people. So it's starting to get normalized for me."

"You *did*?" I ask. "Why didn't you tell me?"

This time she laughs. "Because it's a spinoff of one of my parenting groups, and every time I start talking about the Facebook groups I'm in your eyes glaze over."

"They don't!"

"They do," she says with a playfully patronizing smile. "But that's okay."

"You're just in so many! About so many things! Craft-a-longs and traveling and bodice rippers and I don't even know what else."

"And non-monogamy," she says, and I nod.

"And non-monogamy. Why'd you join?"

She shrugs. "I joined after we had the talk with Bex and Rafael at the restaurant. Because I felt like I needed to be part of a community and not like I was the only person in the world who half-wanted to see what it would be like to try it for real."

"Do you think we're non-monogamous?"

Darcy gives me a *look*.

"Okay, we're non-monogamous. But do you want to open up further than just them?"

At that question Darcy pauses for a moment, thinking, as I pull into our garage. After I turn off the car, I shift so that I'm facing her, and she does the same. "I don't think so? I mean, I'm curious, but I don't think I'm *that* curious. What happened with Bex and Rafael did because of specific circumstances, and I'm not sure I want to seek it out on purpose. Also, it made me realize that at this point in my life I've become a relationship person, and it's complicated enough with them. I don't want to add on other possibilities."

I nod, considering that. "Same, I think. Though I guess I hadn't really thought about the community aspect before."

"It helps," she says with a shrug. "It's one of the things that helps, at least."

"What else helps?" I ask, and this time she grins, crawling over the center console, while I laugh and start pushing my chair back.

"This," she says, straddling my lap, breasts pushed up against my chest in the close quarters of the front seat. "You."

I rest my hands on her thighs, then slip them further up, under her skirt, groaning when I realize she's not wearing anything under her clothes.

"Have you been without panties this whole time?" I ask, and she grins and nods, taking one of my hands and placing it between her legs, covering the warm, wet heat of her. She grinds against my hand and my head drops down to her shoulder. "Fuck. If I'd have known that I'd have finger fucked you during the movie."

"I'd have let you," she whispers, mouth by my ear. "It would have been so good, your hands on my clit, your long fingers working inside me."

"It would have," I agree, finding the little nub and sliding my fingers against it, tracing her opening. "But you would have had to be quiet, and you're not very good at that."

"What if I hadn't?" she asks, moving against my hand. "What if all those noises had slipped out and caught Art and Jen's attention? What if they'd been interested, come back and watched? If they'd have wanted me to, maybe I would have hiked my skirt up for them, spread my legs."

"Would you show off your pretty little pussy for them?" I ask, speeding up a bit. "Do you want to show people how good I am with my hands? Do you want to hump my fingers and let them watch you orgasm? Does that get you hot?"

"I think it would," she says, her breath speeding up. "I'm pretty hot when I orgasm, aren't I? I think there are some people who might enjoy watching it."

"I fucking love it," I say, adding a second finger inside her, then a third. "The way your moans echo off the walls and your tits move up and down with your breath. How you hump whatever you can, whether it's my hand or my face or my cock, and how I can tell when you're getting close because of how desperate you are when you move. And your chest and your face get all flushed because getting off is hard work, and you're a fucking pro at it. Anyone who is lucky enough to see you in this state should be honored, because you're so fucking hot and even just thinking about it makes hard."

"You hard for me right now?" she asks, and I nod as I feel her body start to tense, approach the edge.

"After you come I'm dragging you to our bedroom and fucking you until the kids come home, maybe your mouth, maybe your tits, maybe your pussy, maybe your ass–"

"Maybe all of them?"

"Fuck yes, baby. Come on my hand and then we'll go upstairs and I'll spread you out on our bed. Every inch of you will get my hands or my mouth or my cock or maybe all three."

"All three," she whimpers, and I can tell she's so close, she's right there on the edge. I pull up her shirt, pull a tit out of her bra, attach my mouth to her nipple and suck, hard. The fingers of my free hand dig into her ass while my other hand continues fucking her, refusing to let up until she's satiated.

And then it comes, the grunt, the groan, the loud swearing. The *oh my god* and *fuck so good* and *don't ever stop* that echo against the walls of our garage. And then the slowing of her body, the grip of my wrist to still it, the release of tension and the way her languid body settles against mine. The rhythmic breathing, the peace on her face, the tiny content smile playing on her lips.

"Good?" I ask, and she chuckles and nods.

"Something like that."

"Good," I say.

***

Later that afternoon, half an hour before the kids need to be picked up, we're getting out of the shower, rinsed off from my promise to worship every inch of her. Towel-dried and naked, she throws herself on our messy bed and stretches out, eyes closed.

With my camera I snap a picture and one eye pops open when she hears it.

"For the thread?" she asks, and I shrug and nod.

"Up to you."

"Go for it," she says. It didn't take us long to move from truth or dare to tit and dick pics, and my wife always makes sure to share the porny gifs that she finds. Darcy and I still share some messages just between the two of us, but at least half of what we send goes to the group as a whole, and Bex and Rafael have been keeping up with us.

So I send them her picture, under a string of woman-on-woman gifs that Darcy and Bex traded the other day, and a picture from Rafael that shows off a delicious-looking bulge in his boxer briefs.

Then I settle next to her, one hand on her thigh as I flip through my phone. There's a notification for a text, and after I open and study it, I tilt it in the direction of Darcy. "You were right."

"About?" she asks, shifting so that she's propped up against the pillows and taking the phone out of my hand to read the text.

Art: Hey, just wanted to touch base about earlier. Claudia and my relationship isn't what a lot of people would consider traditional. She knows about Jen and is cool with it, plays hooky sometimes without me also.

She shrugs. "Nice that he told you when he didn't really need to."

"Yeah," I agree, looking at my phone for a long minute before typing out a reply.

Alec: Hey man, thanks for letting me know. No judgement, that's actually what Darcy assumed when she saw you two.

Art: Nice! We haven't gotten "caught" all that often, but one time Claud did and the assumption was cheating and things got messy. So we figured I should out myself just in case, because people don't generally default to thinking that.

I pause for a moment, considering my reply.

"How would you feel about people in our real life knowing? Not who, of course, I wouldn't name names or even enough specifics that people could guess. But, I don't know, you said having people to talk to about it helped?"

She rests her chin on my shoulder, reading the thread. "I think case by case basis on who we tell, but if you want to tell Art I think that's fine?"

When I'm done typing I show her the response and she nods before I press 'enter.'

Alec: Darcy and I have played around with ethical non-monogamy some, have a bit of a situationship going on right now, actually. So kind of nice to know we're not the only ones.

*Art: You're totally not. We're pretty connected with the local
kink scene, so if you ever want to go to a munch or something,
let me know.*

I flip to google and start typing in 'munch' when Darcy supplies the answer for me instead.

"A get together of kinky people, usually at a bar or restaurant or something. Vanilla, just talking and socializing."

"You've done your research!" I say, impressed and also a little surprised.

"I'm a good student," she teases with a wink. "But if you ever wanted to go to one, I'd be down."

"Are you sure you don't want to open up–"

"I don't," she says, cutting me off. "Not right now, at least, not any more open than we already are. But I think meeting more people would be nice. And it's not just poly people, sometimes it's other types of kink, BDSM. There's a swingers club in town and according to the local kink subreddit you can go and just watch or just play with each other, there's no pressure to play with anyone else if you don't want to."

I nod, absorbing all of this, not entirely sure how to respond. This wasn't just one Google while she was bored, it was real research. And not only in the theoretical sense, but looking into what's going on locally, what's actually available to us. "Why didn't you tell me you'd been reading so much about this? To be clear, I'm totally into the fact that you have, but I'm curious why you haven't brought it up."

She shrugs, flushing a bit. "I don't know. It feels kind of weird to admit, I think? Like, I assumed you'd be okay with me researching, might even be interested? But I don't know, admitting it feels like this whole weird big step. And we've already had a few of those recently."

I lean over to press a kiss to her mouth, then rest my forehead against hers. "Definitely interested. And definitely think the fact that you are and you've done research about it is hot."

She grins and gives me another kiss, this one longer and a bit more lingering. "Then tell him we're in."

Alec: We'd love to, keep us in the loop.

October

text messages

Alec: Saw this, thought of you! [chrisandkate.mov]

Bex: Are you sending us porn?!?

Alec: ...yes

Rafael: Bex doesn't watch porn, but I say thanks.

Alec: Wait, Bex, do you really not watch porn?

Bex: Rarely. I wouldn't even know where to start.

Darcy: I mean, I can tell you where to get started if you want to! And this couple is the perfect place, they're a married couple and their whole schtick is authentic, realistic intimacy.
Darcy: But if you don't that's okay too, of course. No pressure.

Rafael: I'm across the room from her and she just turned to me and when I looked back she blushed and looked away.

Darcy: Your wife is too cute. You should have seen how she blushed when she asked me about anal last trip.

Rafael: She STILL blushes sometimes when we talk about it. And when we do it.

Darcy: But the important thing is she's doing something she likes, even if it makes her blush!

Rafael: And she does like it...
Rafael: [fountain.gif]

Bex: I HATE YOU BOTH! Alec, wanna run away together?

Darcy: Hey!

Alec: Sorry babe, pretty sure this is an offer I can't turn down.

Darcy: Was that directed to me, or Rafael?

Alec: Both of you ;)

Bex: ANYWAY if you're asking if there has been penis in

butthole the answer is yes

Darcy: Did you enjoy it enough to do it more than once?

Rafael: [bex.jpg]

Alec: Is hiding your face with your hands a yes or a no?

Rafael: It's a yes.

Darcy: Alec is too polite to ask what's been in Rafael's ass, but I'm not.

Bex: We have not reached coke-can sizes, but we're getting there.

Alec: Just to be clear, coke-can Alec is a nickname, not an exact measurement.

Rafael: Oh, I haven't forgotten the measurements.

Bex: He smirked when he typed that.

Darcy: [RoseSprayBottle.gif]

Bex: Related: have you guys gotten possible dates from grandparents on childcare in March/April? And where are we going?

Alec: Darce did, she'll email. And we're going to this meetup next week and I was going to ask if they had any suggestions.

Rafael: Meetup?

Darcy: Alec found out one of his colleagues is poly, and he invited us to lunch with some of his friends.

Alec: No one will be doing anything, it's a public place and everything, just getting to know people.

Darcy: We're not planning on doing anything, just meeting people.

Alec: We haven't told them the specifics about our situation or anything, either.

Darcy: We obviously aren't going to tell anyone your names or enough details that they could figure it out.

Alec: Now that I think about it we probably should have told you in person. Sorry about that.

Bex: It's fine! I mean I GUESS you're allowed to have friends outside of us. And do the OCCASIONAL social thing outside of us!
Bex: And in all seriousness, we trust you not to share so much

that we're identifiable.

Rafael: Though if you do decide to pursue additional partners we'd want to know, of course.

Darcy: Of course. But we're not.

Alec: We really aren't.

Bex: We trust you.

Rafael: Bex is right, we do.
Rafael: And I hope you have fun

Bex: Also, for the record, the regular cans are definitely too big, but they have those mini ones that aren't totally off.

Alec: Did you just call my cock mini sized?

Bex: Let's go with fun sized instead. Like the candy bars!

Darcy: It's absolutely fun sized.

Rafael: Agreed.

Darcy: Also, Bex, you seem to have given a lot of thought to the size of my husband's cock.

Bex: [kristenbellshrug.gif]

November

darcy

"I DON'T KNOW WHAT to wear!" I say, looking at our bed where I've strewn every item of lingerie I own, and most of my clothes.

"What did your Facebook friends say?" Alec asks as slips into boxers.

"Something that makes me feel sexy. A bodystocking. Nothing with too many buttons or buckles. Club wear. Easy access to boobs if I want you to play with them without getting totally naked."

"So wear that," he says with a shrug, and I groan, pulling out my phone.

Bex's face appears after the first ring.

"Kids around?" I ask.

"One minute, I'll go upstairs. Oh my God, is that every item of clothes you own?" she asks.

"Is that a video call?" Alec asks. "I'm changing!"

"She's seen you naked, it's fine," I tell him, then turn my focus to Bex who is now closing the door to her bedroom. "What do I wear to a sex club?"

"Why are you asking me?" she laughs. "I've never been to one!"

"Yes, but you're the double whammy of finding me irresistible *and* knowing my wardrobe. Alec is only one of those."

"Fiiiine." She says it like she's annoyed, but she's grinning. "That black lace thong you have has a matching bra, right? Start with that."

I prop the phone up on my nightstand and rummage through the clothes on the bed until I find them, then drop the robe I have and pull them on.

"Oooo, I get the pre-show," Bex says, and I grin at her, giving my chest a little shimmy before I put on the bra. She fans herself on the other side of the screen.

"Now what?" I ask.

"Put your husband on the screen."

Alec ducks his head by mine and gives a little wave. "Hey Bex!"

"What dress of Darcy's makes you consider canceling your plans in favor of having her sit on your face all night?" she asks, and I laugh as he gets thoughtful.

"The black one," he says. I'm about to point out that I own multiple black dresses when he surprises me with more detail. "Knee length, thin straps, like this in the front?" He traces what would be a v-neck, and I start digging through the clothes trying to find the one he's talking about.

"It's totally not sexy," I say. "It's just like a cotton summer cocktail dress. It even has pockets."

"Alec, is it sexy?" Bex asks as I find it, holding it up for both of them to see.

Alec grins and nods. "You're totally fuckable in that dress."

"If your plan is just to go there and watch and play with each other, his is the opinion that's most important, right? And even if you change your mind and end up clicking with someone, having a hottie like Alec drooling over you will only make you more attractive."

"Bex thinks I'm a hottie," Alec says, clearly pleased at the news.

I shove him away and pull the dress over my head. Then pick my phone up and I sit on the floor, looking at Bex seriously. "I'm not going to find someone I click with enough that I want to do anything."

She shrugs. "I'm just saying. You're very clickable."

"Would you rather me not go?" I ask. It's a conversation we've already had, first in our text thread with the husbands, and then Bex and I in person. And both times she was very encouraging, said she wanted a full report afterward.

"I wish something like that was in the cards for us," she admitted over coffee last week. "Even if we didn't go with you two, or if we did but didn't play with each other, just with our husbands. But there's still the concern about being seen by someone we know, people finding out."

Bex has been really careful not to ever say that she's more curious and Rafael is more hesitant, but the clues are all there. If Alec and I were also split as far as what to do I wouldn't out him as the reluctant party, so I get that. And I'm sure it's something they're working out between themselves. But I still feel guilty for being able to do stuff that she wants to but isn't doing. It's weird trying to balance everything, to share without feeling like I'm bragging, to sympathize without feeling like we're throwing Rafael under the bus for not wanting to.

"Would you feel more comfortable if I didn't go?" I asked when we talked in person, and she shook her head vigorously.

"No. I feel a little left out, but I still want you to go, want you to have fun, want you to tell me every little detail. I'm living vicariously through you, okay?"

She says the same thing now, over the phone, and I nod. "Want to do brunch tomorrow so that I can dish all the dirt?"

Bex laughs and shakes her head. "You're so not going to be up at a reasonable time tomorrow. We'll catch up next week."

"Love you," I say, and she blows me a kiss, then calls out, "Make sure Alec rolls his sleeves up for forearm porn!"

***

An hour later we're there, and I'm clinging to Alec's hand like it's a lifeline, hoping my nerves aren't obvious to the staff member that's giving us a tour. There's a bar with a dance floor downstairs, and upstairs there are plenty of dark corners, as well as some rooms with windows and others with curtains, all with large beds. They explain that after a room is emptied the staff will clean the room and change the sheets before it's opened back up again.

"Right, great," I say, while inside I realize I hadn't even thought about making sure the sheets are clean, and wonder what I got myself into.

But by the time we're done and go back downstairs the energy is buzzing and I'm feeling less anxious. We grab a table and watch for a bit, then are joined by Alec's colleague Art, and his wife. I wasn't entirely sure how Alec would feel about going to a sex club that his work friend frequented, but he seemed unbothered. "I'd feel weird about either of us hooking up with them," he'd admitted when we talked about it. "But since we're not hooking up with anyone I think it's fine."

At the club, Claudia slips into the booth next to me. "How's your first visit going?"

I shrug, then nod. "Good, I think? Weird. But fun. And hot."

"You're just playing with each other tonight, right?"

Alec nods, and Claudia grins. "Then I won't ask you to dance," she says, winking at me. "But you look great. Love your dress."

"It has pockets!" I say, because I think a woman just hit on me and it's the only thing I can think of to say. And because women can always bond over dresses with pockets.

I'm right that it gives us a bonding point, and Claudia and I talk a bit more before she sees someone she knows across the room and Art joins her.

"If you're done flirting *I* would like to ask you to dance," Alec says.

I flush and take his offered hand as he leads me out to the floor. "I wasn't flirting!"

"You were a little. But it's okay." He drapes my arms around his neck then wraps his around my waist, drawing our bodies together. "It's hot," he whispers, breath hot against my ear, and one hand sides down to my ass, pressing me against him.

I like that I don't have to adjust, move his hand further up and pull away from what feels like the beginnings of a hard-on. That I can shift against him, encourage his erection, catch his ear between my teeth and make him groan softly. We're surrounded by couples, throuples, groups with all combinations of genders, sexuality on display without reservation. No one gives us a second glance, or if they do it's out of desire and interest instead of judgment.

"You're hot," I say, and his hand grips my ass a little tighter, encouraging me to rub up and down his cock as it hardens and lengthens under his pants. "All of you."

"You talking about this ole thing?" he says, and I reach down between us, gripping him over his clothes, giving him a squeeze as his eyes flutter shut.

"Kind of obsessed with your cock," I say, chuckling when my thumb runs over a spot that's just barely damp. It's the energy of this place that got my 43 year old husband so turned on so quickly that he's starting to soak through his clothes. It's pure sex.

"Should we see if there are any rooms available upstairs?"

My heart starts pounding in my chest, but I nod, and he tugs me off the dance floor, toward the stairs. We talked about this, that if we can find a free room with a curtain and it feels right, we want to have sex, but we're not ready to be fully on display. I don't mind people hearing, using their imagination to fill in the blanks, but all our dirty talk aside I don't think I want anyone to actually see us strip down and get it on.

Well, except for Bex and Rafael, of course.

It's not the first time tonight that I've thought of them—we talked about them on the Uber ride over, and at the bar. And as much as I think it would be fun for them to be here, there is a part of me that loves just having Alec, getting to do this with just him. Not getting distracted by Bex's nipples or Rafael's arms. Being able to focus on just my husband is nice. If one day we expand our relationship beyond just the two of us, whether it's with Bex and Rafael, or open it the way Claudia and Art have, I hope we continue to make time for the two of us, and *just* the two of us.

Upstairs the rooms with curtains are taken, so we end up watching two couples having sex on a bed next to each other, swapping partners halfway through. It's incredibly hot, made more so by the soundtrack of people in other rooms, or in dark corners. At one point Alec takes my hand and guides it to his cock, which is as hard as I am wet. I give it a squeeze and he lets out a quiet groan, trying not to take the attention away from the couples on the bed. But he laces his fingers through mine and tugs me away from the room.

A moment later I'm pinned between him and a wall, Alec's mouth on mine. He reaches down for my thigh, urging my leg up and around his waist. When I follow his lead he shifts and settles against me, cock pressing against my pussy in the most perfect way.

Alec's palm runs up and down my thigh, pushing the skirt of my dress up to my waist, and then skimming bare leg until he reaches my knee. "Can I finger you?" he asks. "Or should we save that for when we get home?"

I may not be ready to have sex in public, but I'm down for an orgasm, so I nod, and he grins, hand skimming back up to my ass. His finger traces the line of my thong, between my cheeks then around to my pussy where there's little doubt that I'm wet. And I want him to push the fabric aside, run his finger across my clit, but he doesn't. He cups me with his hand, heel of it making slow circles, but then slides back up my ass again, tracing the fabric to my waist. His finger loops around the string and tugs, lace shifting against my sensitive skin, and it's such a tease, but such a decadent one, and I hook my leg higher around his back, wanting more. Alec lets the fabric slack, and then tugs again, and this time I shift at the same time and the sensation increases. Again and again, I'm basically humping my underwear, humping air, as the fabric slips into my folds and the sensations increase.

I know he's trying to draw it out, he wants me to ask, and I'd planned on holding out but how can I, in this place, surrounded by people and sounds and sensations that all only drive my desire higher? "Please," I finally breathe, and Alec grins.

"Please what?"

"Your fingers, please. Inside me."

Finally his hand slips under the fabric and one finger slides inside me.

And then he stops.

"Alec!" I say, and he plasters an innocent look on his face, which is a talent considering he has one finger inside me and a thumb on my clit.

"Yes?"

"I said stop teasing!"

"You actually didn't," he replies, matter-of-factly, which means he's way more collected than I am. "You just asked for my fingers. And I believe you have them."

My head thumps back against the wall, because he might be right but I can't remember. Everything is hazy except for the feel of his fingers, the knowledge that they could slide against my slick skin with so much ease. And yet they're not.

"Then stop teasing!" I demand, and when he looks at me with a quirked eyebrow I roll my eyes, but add, "Please."

And that's when the finger inside me pumps in and out, thumb circling my clit. My sigh this time is audible, noisy even, and he continues, eventually adding a second and then a third finger.

I'm trying to be quiet but noises are still escaping, and I'm not sure if we're tucked enough into a dark corner that people might not notice. But the not knowing if we're being watched, if *I'm* being watched amps everything up even more, and I rock my lower half against his hand.

"Can I stroke your g-spot?" he asks, knowing any attempts at discretion will be lost if he does, and I nod, because fuck discretion. We didn't come here to be discrete, we came here to watch and be watched, to try something new, to let go.

And let go I do as his finger finds the spot and I whimper, starting to fuck his hand in earnest.

"Fuck," I gasp. "Fuck, Alec, it's so good." And then I lose track of what I'm saying, because I'm so in my body, so focused on this pleasure that's wrapping around me. That's hitting me from the finger on my g-spot and the thumb on my clit and the knowledge that there may be people watching this, getting hard to this, getting wet to this, that later on people may touch themselves to the memory of it. From the knowledge that I'm desirable, that people may want me, but they won't get me, because there's only three people that do, and only one of them is here right now. That Alec is the hottest man I've ever fucked, and this is how he wants to spend his Saturday night, making me come in the dark corner of a sex club. That he's doing this not knowing that my plan is to swallow his cock once I'm recovered, because I love making him come just as much as I love coming. That later tonight we'll fuck until we have no energy left, and that I'm the luckiest person on earth to get to call this man my partner in life.

All of this swirls around me, my whole body tensing, on the edge, movements and noises and everything a blur except for me and Alec.

And then I come.

I'm whimpering and yelling and gasping and continuing to fuck his hand, continuing to draw it out until it's too much and I'm overwhelmed. At some point I realize my cheeks are wet and I'm not sure when or why or how, just that I needed this release so much that tears insisted on being part of it.

Eventually I'm limp and still, pinned between the wall and Alec's body. He's running his thumb on my cheeks, then reaches for a box of tissues that someone put on the table next to us. I dab at my eyes with one, and it comes back black.

"My mascara's running," I say, and there are some quiet chuckles. People along the edges of my vision start to drift away.

"You're gorgeous," Alec says. "Also, I shouldn't have waited this long to get you off in public."

This time I'm the one that laughs, done dabbing at my eyes and resting my forehead on his shoulder. "That was really good."

"I gathered," he says. "And now we're going to get you some Gatorade and go home, because I want you naked as soon as possible."

He's confused when I lift my head and shake it.

"I was going to swallow your cock! Need everyone to see that I give as good as I get!"

He presses a kiss to my mouth. "Need to save something for next time."

I like the sound of that.

"There's going to be a next time?"

Alec nods. "Fuck yes. Tons of them."

December

text messages

Bex: In Costco.

Rafael: Are you texting this in the right place?

Bex: Yes. [pic.jpg]
Bex: Since we're a few months from our next vacation.

Darcy: Oooo, yes. That's my favorite brand of lube, too.

Alec: Buy like six of them.

Bex: I'm not going to be the person in the checkout line at Costco with twelve muffins and six lubes.

Darcy: Why not? People will be so jealous, those muffins are delicious.

Bex: [rolleyes.gif]

Rafael: I don't know that we need SIX, but it probably wouldn't hurt to get a few?

Darcy: Ohhhhhh?

Rafael: For Alec and me.

Darcy: [highFive.gif]

Alec: You're ready?

Rafael: Ready as I'll ever be.

Alec: Sweet.

Darcy: Babe, you need to be more enthusiastic than that. Rafael's being vulnerable over here, he's telling you he wants to fuck. Let's try that again.

Alec: 'bout to start typing one handed at the thought of it.

Bex: Hot.

Darcy: Much better.

Rafael: I would too, but we can't all work from home.

Darcy: Rafael, what have I told you about checking this app at work!

Rafael: To be fair, when it started I thought Bex was going to ask if I needed any new socks from Costco.
Rafael: Also, sometimes I feel left out when you guys are all up in here and I can't be.

Bex: Awww, honey, why didn't you say something?

Rafael: It's fine.

Darcy: Seriously though, if you'd rather us not chat in here at certain times we can stop.
Darcy: You're an integral part of this, and I don't want you feeling like anything less than that.

Alec: Darcy's right.
Alec: We care about you and everything you're feeling. It's important to us.

Rafael: Thanks.
[Rafael is typing...]
[Rafael is typing...]
[Rafael is typing...]
Rafael: I care about y'all, too.

Darcy: [happytears.gif]
Darcy: [grouphug.gif]

Darcy: I mean, we can all agree that this is weird as fuck, but I'm very thankful for it.

Bex: I don't know. Sometimes I think the weirdest part about it is that it's NOT weird.

Alec: How do you mean?

Bex: Just that, objectively, hooking up with your best friend while your husbands watch seems like it should feel weird. But last trip it didn't as much?

Darcy: Yeah. Or like 'Alec sent a naked picture of me to his best friend. Just another Tuesday in my life.'

Rafael: Wait, we're getting another picture of you tomorrow?

Bex: Yeah, I didn't realize it was a Tuesday thing, going to mark it in my calendar.

Darcy: You know what I mean.
Darcy: But also we can make it a Tuesday thing if you just want to see me naked that often.

Bex: I think I'm supposed to say nah in order to keep your massive ego in check, but hormones are taking over and I'm going to say yes please.

Rafael: Is it still hormones when you're pushing 40?

Alec: Shot across the bow from the baby of the group!

Darcy: Didn't think about the fact that you're in a May-December situation with BOTH your fuck buddy AND your wife.

Bex: Hey, I'm only 6 months older, Alec's got us beat by THREE YEARS.

Darcy: He's starting to walk around with a cane.

Alec: That's not a cane, that's my cock. Though I understand how you got the two confused.

Bex: Speaking of coke cans...

Rafael: Ahh, this is how it all comes full circle. I was wondering if that was going to happen.

Darcy: Wait, Bex, are you sexting in the aisles of Costco?

Bex: I was, now I'm sexting from the parking lot. And I need to get home before school pickup, so I'll chat with you pervs later.
Bex: [blowkisses.gif]

January

bex

I'M IN THE BATHROOM, washing my face, when my phone vibrates. Then vibrates again. And a third time. In the bedroom I can hear Rafe's doing the same thing, rattling against his nightstand.

"What am I missing out on?" I ask, not wanting to stop in the middle of my skincare routine, because I know if I do I'll probably end up dropping the habit for the next six months until I remember again.

"Just Darcy," he calls back. "Spamming the chat with DP gifs."

"Of course she is," I say with a laugh.

A few minutes later, after digging through Rafe's drawers and finding a t-shirt of his that's soft enough to sleep in, I slip into bed beside him and open up our group thread. Sure enough, there are about fifteen new gifs to scroll through. *Hot* I reply, then snuggle down in bed and look at them more closely.

"I like how you say you don't really like porn, but have no issue with porn gifs," Rafe teases, and I shrug, because honestly, he's right.

"Darcy's good at picking the ones that I think are hot. I'm sure there are tons that I *wouldn't* be into, but I let Darcy cultivate a selection. Like, look at this one." It's a picture of a woman riding a man and kissing him, while another man stands behind her and fucks her in the ass. "It's obviously porn, but it doesn't feel gratuitous? Or... I don't know how to explain it. It's just hot."

"Are you developing a curiosity about DP?" he asks me, rolling me on my side and pressing himself against my ass.

"Nah," I say, sweeping my hair down and stretching my neck out in the hopes that he'll pay it some attention. "Anal alone is still a novelty for me, two men would be way overwhelming."

"Mmmmm," he says, taking my hint and pressing kisses along my neck. I relax against him, letting my eyes flutter shut.

"How about you?"

His lips freeze on my collar bone for just a moment, then he clears his throat. "How about me what?" he asks, even though it's obvious from his reaction that he understood my question.

I look over my shoulder at him. "Are you interested in double penetration?"

"I don't have two holes," he says, attempting to duck down again, but I pull away, rolling over to face him, and wondering why he's being so avoidant.

"You know what I mean. Would you be interested in... whatever the terminology is. Double penetrating someone?"

"Does it matter if you're not?"

He's refusing to meet my eyes, so I push myself up to sitting, facing him and raising my eyebrows. Finally, he says something.

"I mean, sure. I'm curious."

"If Darcy and Alec—" I start, but he cuts me off.

"No, we don't do that."

That's why he's so avoidant. Because he wants to, but doesn't think he should.

"Eighteen months ago there was a lot we didn't do that we do now. Things change."

He shakes his head, shoulders tense. "I can't fuck your best friend."

"Why not?" I ask, and he throws his hands up in the air.

"You realize how ridiculous you sound, right?"

And he's not wrong, but he's also not completely right. Considering what we've been doing, what we're going to be doing again in a couple of months, the conversation we're having isn't completely out of left field.

"A little," I admit. "But you still haven't answered my question."

His voice is low when he asks, "What if I like it?"

"Rafe. I'm not suggesting it in the hopes that you hate it."

"So why *are* you suggesting it?"

I shrug, and take a moment to consider the question. Because the me of two years ago would have completely blanched at the knowledge that I'd be open to my husband having a threesome with my best friend and her husband. But things change.

"Because I love you, and I care a lot about Darcy, and I think Alec's pretty great, and if there's something that three of you want to try, I want to encourage you to try it. If I really wanted to try with you and Alec, would you be down for it?"

"Yeah," he admits.

"Even though it would mean your best friend is fucking me?"

"It's different."

"It really isn't."

Rafe rubs his eyes with his hands. "I can't believe we're discussing this."

"There's a lot about our life these days I can't believe."

"It just... feels like I shouldn't. Shouldn't want to, shouldn't do it, shouldn't *any* of it." Again, his voice is quiet. Serious.

I shift to my knees, placing my hands on his cheeks and pressing a quick kiss to his mouth. "I'm tired of things feeling wrong because everyone tells us they're wrong. Fucking my best friend, watching you fuck yours, orgies in the shower, even anal. How about we trust each other to ask for what we want, knowing that if the other person isn't okay with it they'll say no?"

"Yeah," he says quietly, and I know he hasn't come around yet, but that I'm making him think. And that's a good place to stop for now, because I don't want to push him too far.

"Sleep on it," I tell him. "Try and figure out if you're saying no because you don't want to, or because you think you're not supposed to want to."

He nods.

"Also," I say. "We're a few weeks away from our next trip, and I think there's other stuff we should talk about before then."

The way his gaze immediately drops to his hands shows me he knows what I'm talking about.

"We don't have to talk about your attraction to Darcy if that's too much. But I think we should talk about how you're feeling about Alec."

He takes a deep breath and finally looks up at me. "Not tonight though?"

I nod. "Not tonight. But soon?"

He nods again.

***

The next day, after we tuck in our youngest and our older two are in their rooms for the night, Rafe and I settle on the couch to watch tv. But before I can turn it on, he shifts to face me.

"What if I really like him?"

He doesn't give me more context than that, but I know what he's talking about anyway. I've been anxiously waiting for this conversation for the past seven months–since we got back from the last trip, and had the discussion that led to that awkward double date—and now it's time.

"I think I'm starting to more than like Darcy," I admit.

His nod doesn't come as a surprise to me. We both know better than anyone what we look like when we're falling in love.

"It's scary," I continue. "Because it doesn't affect how I feel about you, but if I nurture it, who knows."

"Yeah," he agrees. "So do we stop? Cancel the trip?"

No! I yell internally, because that's the last thing I want. But it's also probably the logical thing to do. So I turn it back on him. "Would you feel more comfortable if we did?"

"Fuck if I know," he says, burying his face in his hands. I rub his back, and we both let the silence settle around us for a few minutes, until he finally speaks again. "I know I'm the one holding you back."

"What do you mean?"

He lifts his head and turns to look at me. "If I hadn't had concerns, would you and Darcy have spent time together since the last trip? Would we have actually tried polyamory, and not just friends with benefits?"

Rafe is right, I would have. "Your concerns aren't holding me back, though. You're always more important to me, and I only want to do this if we're both fully on board. I'm not risking our marriage over this, I've never even considered it."

"Still," he says. "Is me being scared really a good enou–"

I interrupt him with a vehement, "Yes. *Any* reason is good enough."

He takes my hand with both of his, playing with it. Tracing my palm, the lines on each of the joints on my fingers. Flips it over and strokes my knuckles.

Then he takes a deep breath.

"Hypothetical question. What's the point of no return?" Before I can for clarification, his words start tumbling out. "If on this next trip you let yourself like her–*more* than like her, and I let myself more than like him? We try threesomes and whatever else. If we do that, and if one of us decides it's not okay, or if one of *them* decides it's not okay, then what?"

"Then we stop?" I shrug. "I mean, that was always the deal."

"It just feels like there's going to come a point where we can't stop. Where it becomes a thing in and of itself. There'll come a point where I'll no longer be able to say 'I know you love Darcy, but I can't do this anymore.' Or you'll no longer be able to ask that of me."

"Aren't we already kind of there though? If I were to say, 'I can't do this, Rafe, I want to cancel this trip. How would you feel?"

He's confident when he answers, "I'd do it."

"I know you'd do it, that's not what I asked. I asked how you'd *feel*."

"Frustrated," he admits. "But I would still–"

"I know," I say again. "I'm just saying we're already at the point where breaking it off would hurt, where we have to trust each other to be honest with our needs and wants. We already know that we can get through whatever this situation we're in throws at us as a couple. Is taking another step really going to make that big of a difference, considering where we are right now?"

Rafe rubs his forehead with his hand as he shakes his head. "No."

I don't say anything, but inside my heart is pounding, and I feel a little like I'm going to throw up. Because Rafe is right, this *is* scary. Rafe might love Alec. I'm already well on my way to loving Darcy. How to handle this isn't anything I've seen first-hand in the marriages and relationships I know. And I can read *Polysecure* and *Ethical Slut* until I have them memorized, but trying to figure out the extent to which we want to live it is still scary as fuck.

"You'd really be okay with me having sex with Darcy?" he asks, and I both shrug and nod.

"Depending on the situation? I wouldn't be okay with you and her going into another room and closing the door—that feels too intimate. But if you joined her and Alec? Or if she joined you and me? Yeah, I think so."

"Even if I liked it?"

This answer's easy. "If you *didn't* like it, I'd want you to stop. When I'm asking if you'd be interested, I'm asking if you think you'd like it. That's the whole point."

"Would you have sex with Alec?"

Suddenly I understand his insecurity about admitting that he thinks he'd like having sex with Darcy. Still, I swallow down my nerves and choose honesty. "I think that could be fun, if everyone was okay with it. Darcy and Alec seem like a good time in bed. And if he joined us and I got your arms *and* his abs?"

He chuckles as he leans over to press a quick kiss to my mouth. Then he reaches for his phone, flipping to the thread we have with them and scrolling through our conversations, our teasing, our pictures and gifs.

"Okay, let's do it," he says.

"Wait, now?" I ask, heart pounding.

"Let's offer Darcy a threesome. Alec too, maybe."

And suddenly I'm the one who's hesitant. "What if they say no? What if they don't like us as much as we like them."

"Rebecca," he says, putting his phone down and looking at me.

"What?"

"There is zero chance of that. The only way Alec would turn down the opportunity to have sex with you is if Darcy wasn't okay with it. That's why I've been so nervous. Because as soon as I say the word it's done." He takes a deep breath. "But I think I'm ready to say the word."

"But what does that mean," I ask, wringing my hands. "If I'm having sex with another man and you're having sex with another woman and we're in love with other people?"

Rafe shrugs, looking a bit uncertain, but pushes past it. "Like you said, we're already past the point of no return, except it's not no return. It's just *painful* return. But regardless, we're there, I don't think this is going to be a huge shift if this trip we add something new to the repertoire."

He's making sense—which, considering he's just echoing back my words to me of course I'd think that. But it seems logical that considering the last two trips, this doesn't seem like it would be a gravitational shift in our relationship.

"Okay," I say slowly.

"So should I text them?"

I nod.

Rafe: Have you and Alec talked about whether you'd be interested in finding a second dude to help you live out your DP dreams?

Less than a minute later my phone vibrates, but Rafe's doesn't. I look, and it's a message from Darcy, without the husbands included.

Darcy: Is your husband propositioning me?

Bex: I think technically he's propositioning both of you.

Darcy: And you're okay with this?

Bex: Yeah. We talked about it before he sent his text.

Darcy: Would you want to be the meat in a me and Alec sandwich?

Bex: Of all of the ways of putting that...

Darcy: That's not an answer!
Darcy: To be clear, it's not an offer because Alec's at a work thing tonight so I haven't discussed any of this with him. But it's not like I've never wondered.

Why does that question feel so vulnerable? My stomach twists and I show my screen to Rafe, who nods encouragingly.

Bex: If asked, yes.

She doesn't answer, and I start to wonder if that was the wrong answer. If they think Rafe offered in the hopes that they would offer in return, because that's something he or I really want, a threesome with them. If this looks like we were trying to choreograph something for our benefit. My stomach is fully in roller coaster mode, up and down and upside down as I stare at my answer and the lack of response.

Then both of our phones vibrate. I glance at Rafe, who still has the thread with all four of us up.

> *Darcy: Alec isn't here, but we'll talk about it tonight/tomorrow? It might be fun to consider sandwiches of all sorts, not just a Darcy sandwich?*

> *Rafe: We're good for that conversation if y'all are.*

> *Darcy: Great. We'll let you know.*

Rafe looks at me. "Now what?"

I shrug. "Now, we wait."

He nods, then starts the show we sat down to watch. But five minutes in I realized I'm not paying any attention at all, because I'm so distracted by the phone and wondering when Alec gets home and if they'll discuss it tonight.

Standing, I take Rafe's hand and tug. "Come on."

"What are we doing?" he asks, standing, and then following me as I lead him to the bedroom.

"Distracting ourselves until they reply."

He grins, then reaches over to snap my bra. "I'm up for that."

And an hour and a half later, after we're done and recovered and Rafe has gotten up to grab me a glass of water, I notice my phone has a notification.

Alec: We're in.

Thank You, Readers!

As a reader, deciding to get emotionally invested in a not-yet-completed series, especially one from a new author, can feel risky. Will they finish the series, or will I have to live the rest of my life not knowing what happened to Bex, Rafe, Darcy, and Alec?!

So, THANK YOU for taking the risk on me and my books. I've loved writing about these four, and I hope that you've loved reading about them.

For indie authors such as myself, reviews are hugely helpful in helping books find their readers, so I'd love if you could leave one on Amazon, Goodreads, Storygraph, and/or anywhere else you tend to buy books!

While you were reading, if you were dying to know what happened when Bex and Rafe disappeared for their own experimentation, I have a short outtake of what happened in their room. You can get it by signing up for my newsletter at https://www.gemmablythe.com/booty

If you're wondering WHAT HAPPENS NEXT?! ALEC SAID THEY WERE IN!! Don't worry, I'm working on book 3, Awakening Affection! Signing up for my newsletter can make sure you get updated when it's up for preorder, likely in the second half of 2024.

And thank you AGAIN, for spending some time with me and my characters!

Acknowledgements

THE VERY FIRST THANKS I want to give are to anyone who has read my words–either in book form, in Vella, or on Radish. I wasn't entirely sure if anyone else would find my horny little stories as fun as I do, and I feel so lucky that my stories have found some readers. Every time you read an episode, buy a book, leave a rating or a review, or talk about it on your socials, my heart grows two sizes.

Once I'd dabbled with Bex's story enough to decide I was going to make a book out of it, my next decision was that it was going to be a four-book series, one told from the point of view of each main character. And I was worried when I first started writing Darcy's story, because I didn't want her to read as Bex as a blonde instead of brunette, but she ended up coming more easily than I expected.

Still, second books are hard, and my critique partners Sarah T. Dubb, Jessica Joyce, and Livy Hart kept me going with encouraging comments and notations on my manuscript, questions that made me think about the story and where it was going, and suggestions that really helped me solidify what I wanted to do with the story. I'm so incredibly thankful for the three of them–they are the reason this book (and the last one, and the next two!) exists.

Once I was done with the first draft, Carla G. gave me some great immediate feedback, and Katheryn Ferrer gave me some thoughts as someone who hadn't read Breaking Boundaries. More thanks go out to my beta readers Mae Bennet, Andrea Rinaldi-Perez, Scarlette Tame, and Vienna Veltman, and my proofreaders Morgan Jones, Jenny Adams and Jenny Lane.

Rae Douglas has been a huge support, answering questions I had, directing me where I can research more, and doing both authenticity and line edits. Her knowledge of spice, polyamory, and kink, is so wonderful, and I'm so lucky to have found her!

I'm super thankful for my online communities–Smutfest 2.0 and Hopefully Writing, who understand the struggle and are a wonderful place to get support.

Shoutouts to my real-life support systems: Carrie, Dani, Elana, and JH, and Jenni, Marci, Meredith, Nate, and Sara, and my kickass neighbor June. Thanks to my parents for promising never to read these books, and to my kids who occasionally ask why I close my google docs as soon as they enter the room.

And to Will. I am truly The Luckiest.

About the Author

Gemma Blythe writes stories about love and relationships: the good, the messy, and the honest. Her love of romance blossomed in high school when unrequited crushes led her to seek happily ever afters in books and movies.

Though Gemma's stories are fiction, she's inspired by the partner she eventually found her own happily ever after with. When Gemma isn't writing, you can find her lost in the pages of a book, cooking up a storm in the kitchen, attempting to interpret her Tarot spread, and trying to convince her friends and family that she would definitely win Survivor. (She would definitely not win Survivor.)

You can find her online at www.gemmablythe.com and keep in touch with her via her newsletter at www.gemmablythe.com/newsletter

www.ingramcontent.com/pod-product-compliance
Lightning Source LLC
Chambersburg PA
CBHW061529310726
48972CB00008B/2376